THE HARD MEN

When Soderstrom advertised for riders the good people of Mimbreno laughed. Who would be stupid or crazy enough to side with Soderstrom against Loftus Buckmaster, the man who ruled the immense Wagontree spread, the town, and the country with an iron-hard fist.

Three men answered the ad. Each had a reason for hating Buckmaster and everything he stood for. Soderstrom recognized this hatred and knew he had found what he needed to even the odds...

A

THE HARD MEN

T. V. Olsen

First published by Barker

This hardback edition 2001
by Chivers Press
by arrangement with
Golden West Literary Agency

ISBN 0 7540 8132 X

British Library Cataloguing in Publication Data available

Printed and bound in Great Britain by
Redwood Books, Trowbridge, Wiltshire

The
HARD
MEN

One

Rocking on its creaking thoroughbraces, the stage rolled to a stop by the stage depot. The four passengers filed off. First to step down was the seedy-looking drummer with bad nerves, clutching his sample case like a talisman. He was followed by a big, rawboned man in a dusty suit of old-fashioned cut, who then formally handed down a plump blonde woman with knowing eyes. She leaned close to the big man before letting go of his hand, giving him a heavy scent of the perfume that had stifled him for the last twenty miles.

"Well, a gentleman," she murmured huskily and smiled. "You ever come by Maudie's place, and that's one block down, you ask for . . ."

Her voice faded as she met the man's eyes directly for the first time, eyes that reflected no feeling as personal as indignation or even scorn. She took a step backward and whispered, "Excuse me," then brushed past him and walked to the rear boot to receive her luggage from the driver.

Not sparing her another glance, the big man gave a hand to the fourth and last passenger who now stepped from the coach. This was a girl in her late teens, small but not slight of build; the sturdy fullness of her mocked the drab and soiled dress she wore. It was made of a cheap material that matched the frayed traveling cape she carried over one arm and the little dilapidated straw hat that topped the heavy wealth of her whitegold hair. Her face was a pretty one, oval and strong-boned; her young smooth skin had a fine translucence, a milky freshness with a tint of budding roses, but her one really beautiful feature was her eyes. As remarkable as the big man's eyes, they were totally different—warm and wide

7

open, clear as gray crystal, and so honest that meeting them made a man think uncomfortably of forgotten sins.

She said now, with a smile that was curious and faintly chiding, "Papa, what did that woman say?"

"Nothing for your ears," the big man said gruffly. "You have the list I made, Thera? Of the things we will need, eh?"

The girl gave a little sigh, opening the shabby reticule she carried. "Here it is, Papa. But I thought we could get some rooms at the hotel now."

"We will rest when we are home, not before," Krag Soderstrom said brusquely. "There is a general merchandise store across the street. Have the list filled, girl, while I do the other things."

As Thera started across the street, the driver who was unstrapping luggage lashed to the coach top called down, "Mister, you want to help me with this trunk?"

Soderstrom started to turn, and then his gaze was snapped back to the street by a sudden rattle of sound. An instant later six horsemen thundered around the corner of the hotel adjacent to the stage depot, veering in a hard-riding body down the center of the street.

There was no hesitation, or even pause for thought between Soderstrom's awareness of the coming riders and his movement. He took three long steps to reach his daughter. She was halfway across the street when he caught her by the shoulders and dragged her back with a rough power that swung her feet clear of the ground. The riders surged past with a savage momentum, voicing high wild whoops.

Krag Soderstrom drew a deep angry breath, tasting the haze of bitter dust that hung in the air. He said harshly, "You are all right?"

"Yes, all right," Thera said calmly, but she winced as she passed a palm over her upper arm where his fingers had cruelly bruised her.

"That hurt, eh? Not so much as getting rode down, I think."

She smiled at his unyielding gruffness. "No, Papa. Now I will do the shopping."

Soderstrom grimly waited till she had crossed the street and entered the store. He turned to the driver, nodding at the half-dozen riders as they piled off their horses in front of the Alhambra Saloon a block down. "Who are those fools?"

The driver spat over his shoulder, saying, "Wagontree men," as if it explained everything. "Good men. Would of been right sorry if they had rode down your little gal. Here, take aholt on your trunk."

Grunting, he heaved one end of the big brassbound leather trunk over the side rail, and Soderstrom clamped his long arm around it and shifted it easily to his shoulder. Walking slowly but straight as a pine under a burden that had taxed the strength of the two men who had loaded it, Soderstrom tramped into the depot. There he asked for and received permission from the agent to leave behind the ticket counter the trunk which contained all of his and Thera's belongings except the clothes on their backs.

Afterward he stood on the depot's rickety steps and passed his iron glance across the ramshackle cluster of frame and adobe buildings that made up Mimbreno. It was no different from a dozen other sunbaked, sprawling hamlets he had come through in the last few days, and only the fact that it marked the journey's end made it deserving of his particular attention. A hot wind passed up the dusty ribbon of street and riffled the tired leaves of the few cottonwoods drooping in the forenoon heat. A pair of loafers drowsing in barrel chairs on the hotel veranda gave him a lazily curious scrutiny.

Krag Soderstrom's size alone would mark him even in this land where big, hard, and weathered men were no exception. His heavy-boned body towering inches above most men carried little excess flesh, and at thirty-seven, despite his near-ungainly size and build, all his movements had the effortless grace imparted by superb musculature. He had a long Scandinavian face, squarish and bony, with a rumpled mane of flaxen hair and a ragged pale mustache whose drooping points hid his upper lip. His jaw shelved out like a granite ledge, and his sharp high cheekbones and craggy nose might have been chipped from the flank of a mountain. His eyes, under a straight ridge of whiteblond brows, were an ice-blue so penetrating that few people could bear their direct glance. But that frozen quality went deeper than surface; it tunneled from the cold irises into the inner man in a way that shook and repelled perceptive strangers.

Having taken his bleak, totally unimpressed look at the town, Soderstrom came off the veranda and swung briskly upstreet toward the newspaper building he had noted as the stage rolled in. His walk was hampered by the tightness across chest and shoulders of his old wedding suit which he had hardly worn in eighteen years. Now it was wrinkled and dust-creased by long days and nights on cross-country trains and coaches, and his boiled white shirt was smudged and stale, the high stiff collar wilted by sweat. Soderstrom had never sweated so much in his life. It was the dead simmer of oppressive heat, and not the jolting discomfort of a long journey broken only by fitful snatches of sleep, that laid a dull exhaustion on his northlander's constitution and temperament. That, and the vagrant currents of loud talk and explosive laughter from the Alhambra across the way, did nothing to improve his always dour temper.

The newspaper was a narrow single-story 'dobe building wedged between two larger ones; the lower half of its big front window was painted white to banner the black block wording, BUCKMASTER COUNTY WEEKLY PRESS. JOB PRINTING. H. KINGERY, ED. AND PROP. Entering, Soderstrom paused inside the doorway. The long gloomy room was a scene of monumental order and disorder. The side walls were piled with a clutter of boxes and cartons and yellowing stacks of newspapers. To his left was an iron safe and a clothes commode, to his right a swivel chair and a desk heaped with neatly stacked papers and proofs. The room was divided midway by a wooden railing, and from the print shop at the rear came a curious, steady sound of metal striking metal.

A man, short and hunched and white-haired, swinging a stiffed-up leg, was sweeping the floor with slow, jerky movements. His back was to the door, and now as he turned Soderstrom saw that his nut-brown face was networked with wrinkles and scars. His eyes had the blankness of pale blue marbles, and something not quite definable in his look made a man's flesh crawl.

"You want something?" His scarred lips contorted in forming speech.

"You are the owner?"

The man gave an inarticulate mutter and tilted his white head toward the rear, then went on sweeping. Soderstrom went across the office and through the railing gate. As he circled a tall cabinet he removed his old slouch hat. Behind the cabinet a young woman was seated on a high stool. She was wearing a drab and worn workdress and an ink-stained apron, and her right hand moved with deftness and speed as she selected type from two cases set on a sloping frame and slapped it into a stick in her left hand.

Without looking up, she said evenly, "Well, what do you want?"

"I want to place an ad."

"It had better be a short one. We go to press this afternoon and the forms are almost filled." She set down the composing stick and picked up another, looking at him for the first time. He was used to people's half-startled scrutinies at first meetings, but she gave him only a cool appraisal.

She was about twenty-eight, a willowy woman with hair that was a flaming red even in its tight bun under the dim overhead lamp. Her face was angular and clean-lined, with a liberal dusting of freckles across the nose and cheeks; she was far from pretty, but definitely not plain.

She looked tired and slightly harried, and now she said irritably, "Well?" He looked at her blankly, and the faintest smile touched her wide mouth. "I can set type as fast as you dictate. Go ahead."

"Wanted," Soderstrom said, and paused to watch her ink-stained fingers blur into motion. A moment later she looked up, and he went on, "Experienced riders. Forty a month and keep—"

"Thirty."

"What, missus?"

"Thirty a month is the going rate in these parts."

"All right," Soderstrom said coldly. "Apply K. R. Soderstrom, Ladder Ranch."

11

Her fingers ceased movement and she looked up with open curiosity, half-pointing the stick at him. "You're Soderstrom?"

He nodded stiffly; this young woman's manner was too forward to be seemly. And what sort of work was this for a woman?

"Then I take it old Angus Horne has sold Ladder to you."

"That is right. We met at a Grange convention in Minneapolis. There we talked, and the deal was made."

She nodded. "I knew that old Angus had gone to live with his son on a farm up north. Then you're not from Wisconsin, Mr. Soderstrom?"

"There are a few Swedes in Minnesota, too," Soderstrom said gruffly.

That drew a merry, gamin laugh from her as she gave him her hand. "Do excuse my manners, sir. I'm Hannah Kingery, and I own this newspaper."

A half-conscious scowl of stolid disapproval touched his long face, even as he noted the surprising strength of her grip. Her slenderness belied a sturdy robustness, but the fact deepened his disapproval; a fine strong woman like this should be busy with keeping house and bearing children.

Hannah Kingery said quietly, "You wear your opinion of independent women even more frankly than most men, I should say."

Soderstrom grunted, "That is your husband's concern, missus, not mine."

"My husband is dead," she said evenly, and turning back to the typecases, completed the composition of his ad with a brisk deftness. "That will be two dollars."

Soderstrom took out his shabby purse and counted out the coins. As he raised his eyes on handing over the money, he surprised a mounting curiosity in her face, and then she said, "I don't mean to be rude, but could you tell me a couple of things without scowling?"

Soderstrom scowled. "What are they?"

"I was just wondering—I presume you have had experience at ranching?" Her tone presumed that he had none.

"I worked on a cattle outfit in Dakota Territory when I was a kid. Four, five months."

12

"Oh, I see. Four, five months." She hitched her feet to a higher rung on the stool and awkwardly crossed her arms on her knees. "Second, how much did you pay Angus Horne for his Ladder, sight unseen?"

Soderstrom eyed her darkly. "Five thousand dollars for a few thousand acres good riverbottom grass, a ranch headquarters developed already, and about nine hundred head branded stock. The price was plenty low, all right, but Mr. Horne's son is a good friend of mine. His word I take that this is a good outfit." He paused deliberately. "What you think, missus, is you are talking to one big dumb squarehead, eh?"

Not squareheaded, narrowminded," Mrs. Kingery said sweetly. "No, you hardly impress me as stupid. Which increases the puzzle, unless old Angus neglected to bring up a point. Or did he mention Wagontree?"

"Wagontree and the Buckmasters," Soderstrom said stolidly. "I will take care of anything they want to start."

"Oh, indeed. Well, well." She nodded gravely and tapped the composing stick against her chin, leaving a smudge there. "Angus was pushing seventy, of course, and fed up with trouble. That's why he pulled his stakes from here. Perhaps he thought that he could pass his problems on to a younger man in clear conscience. Though if you'll forgive my saying so—"

"I know," Soderstrom grunted. "I'm green as grass, I ain't dry behind the ears, and Loftus Buckmaster is half mustang and half bull buffalo."

"Then old Angus did give you fair warning." A faint smile tugged at her lips, and she was about to say more when the hunched white-haired man came around the cabinet, still clutching the broom.

"Anythin' else you want tended to, Miss Hannah?"

"That will be all today, Waco." Her voice was gentle; she jingled Soderstrom's coins in her palm and impulsively handed them to the white-haired man. "Here. A small bonus, and please—buy yourself one good meal before you start drinking."

"Thankee, Miss Hannah." The man gave Soderstrom a vacant, incurious glance, then went to the wall, leaned his broom there, took a ragged coat from a hook and shuffled out.

"A case in point," Hannah Kingery murmured. "That poor wreck is Waco Millard. He used to be the best bronc-buster in the valley. Now he ekes out a bare living swamping out saloons and stables and the like."

"So?"

"He worked for Loftus Buckmaster, breaking rough string mustangs. One day when Waco was sick, Loftus made him top a killer mustang—it was that or lose his job. The horse threw him, but Waco got a foot hung in a stirrup and the brute bolted through a gate that some fool had left partly open. It was five minutes before a rider was able to overtake the horse." She grimaced faintly, as if at some firsthand memory. "Waco was broken up pretty badly, but Dr. Enever pulled him through, no thanks to Loftus Buckmaster. He had no use for a stove-up hand, and he discharged Waco on the spot with what he had earned to the day, not a penny more."

Soderstrom gave a bleak grunt. "That's plain sense anyhow."

Her eyes clearly mirrored her shock. "Do you mean that as it sounds? That years of loyal service to a brand should count for no more than—"

"Look, missus," Soderstrom cut in harshly. "A man looks out for his own. Good or bad, another man's luck is his own lookout. He has got coming what he earns, not a cent more or less." He arced a callused thumb against his chest. "Me, Krag Soderstrom, I come out here to raise cows, to look out for my own, to tend to my business. That's the way it should be. If this Buckmaster knows that, good. If he don't, maybe he will find out fast."

"Your position is clear enough," Mrs. Kingery said coldly. "I can see that I was wasting my breath. Loftus Buckmaster owns half this valley and is well on his way to taking the rest. In the process he has destroyed a number of people, not by murder. By worse—killing dreams and hopes. Well, perhaps it takes one to oppose one. I wish you not luck but good hunting. You are the same kind of man."

Soderstrom's ice-blue gaze held on her face. "Maybe you will spell that out. What kind of man?"

"Why should you wonder," she retorted with thrusting irony, "if you know yourself as well as you obviously do?

Then you know your enemy. But, very well—Loftus Buck-master is a man who fought Apaches, rustlers, drought, to carve out a piece of God's earth for himself—the trouble being that he got a taste for carving and could not learn to stop. The times he knew, rough and brutal times to be sure, turned him as hard as stone, as if that were any excuse."

"You think it is not, eh?"

"Not," she countered flatly, "unless a man lets it be. Loftus Buckmaster drove the one person who loved him, his wife, to her grave. He pushed his only daughter into making a bad marriage in her simple desperation to get away from him. He made—is still making—his two sons into his own spittin' image. All that is really mild stuff next to his treatment of non-relatives ... all of the little people he's bullied and terrorized. That, of course, is no concern of yours, except as it bears on the fact that you just wasted two dollars."

"Wasted?"

"For the ad. I doubt there is even one rider in Buckmaster County who will dare answer it. Well, even if your days are numbered, I hope you prove mean enough to hurt him even a little—that will make it worth it."

Wondering at the bitter vehemence with which she spoke Soderstrom said, frowning, "This is Buckmaster you're talking about?"

She gave a low, brittle laugh. "I would rather not admit why, but the fact provokes its own admission. Loftus Buckmaster is my father." Briskly she swung back to the typecases, saying matter-of-factly, "If you'll excuse me, I have a form to complete. Your advertisement will appear in today's paper. Good day."

Soderstrom clamped on his hat and tramped toward the front office. He was halfway across the room when he caught a faint, muffled cry from somewhere outside.

That was Thera. Even as the thought crossed his mind he was quickening pace, and three running steps carried him out to the street.

Two

While the elderly storekeeper filled her order, rummaging stiffly among the stacks of goods on shelves and counters, Thera Soderstrom peered out the window at the currents of life on the main street. A great curiosity was in her, mingling with her high excitement. Her zest for life had never been remotely satisfied by her seventeen sheltered years on a little Minnesota farm. Now, within two short weeks thrust into totally new surroundings and situations, her lively young mind was still dazzled by all she had seen, and she could not take in enough of it.

This was Saturday, and now as the morning wore on, the street and sidewalks bustled with the increasing traffic. She was surprised at the number of cowboys thronging the town, wondering why they were not at work; but she remembered how in sawmill towns in the northern woods the lumberjacks would flock in for a payday spree. The sight of so many young Western men quite took Thera's breath away; somehow they seemed invested with a glamour she had never associated with loggers. Almost every one of them was decked out fit to kill, in spanking clean shirts and silk scarves and tight boots so pinch-toed it seemed they must cause the wearers untold miseries. They strutted and swaggered whenever a town belle, high-nosed and parasoled, went by; Thera smiled . . . *They look different, that is all; they are not, really.*

There was one difference: the guns. Although most of the workaday cowhands were unarmed, or wore their pistols stuck in the waist bands of their overalls, a few carried their six-guns in holsters slung from cartridge-studded belts, and she could not help thinking that the more hard-bitten individuals were really of a different breed.

16

Thera's glance was drawn to the doorway of the stage depot as her father stepped out and headed upstreet with his long, swinging stride. She watched his tall, big-shouldered form till he turned into the newspaper office, and then she sighed, a small sadness tucking the corners of her full lips. How lonely he always looked, even in a crowd; she saw what others did not because she remembered and she knew. Krag Soderstrom had always been a gruff and brief-spoken man, that was simply his way, but she could remember, when *Mor* was alive, how Papa's chill eyes had sometimes lightened and danced with flecks of humor. Yes, she could remember, but not very well, for that had been a long time ago.

When the storekeeper had assembled the articles on her list and she had paid him, she asked whether she might leave them there until her father had bought a wagon on which to load their goods. He agreed readily.

Thera was not beautiful, but her smile was; it was like the goodness of sun and wind on a rippling field of ripe wheat, so rich and full that a man's fading eyes stung with the memories, real or fancied, that it provoked.

She thanked him and went out the door, her eyes bent downward as she restored her change purse to her reticule. A man's arm jostled hers in passing, knocking the reticule from her hands.

"Beg par'n, miss," the young man murmured as he paused, bending to pick it up. He doffed his hard derby with a sweep as he handed her the reticule with a crooked little grin. Thera smiled back, her frank gaze admittedly liking him; he was almost as tall as Papa, but very thin, and his shabby slopshop trousers and coat, the latter opened to a frayed dark turtleneck sweater, were a disreputable match for his age-tarnished derby. But she was a little alarmed that such a nice face could have its fine clean lines so stressed by thinness and pallor.

"Thank you," she murmured, and the young man seemed to start when he met her eyes, then lower his own in shame. She saw him stumble as he walked away, and realized with a swift shock that he was drunk. *Oh—poor young man!* He had been drunk long and often, that was plain from his sickly look.

Flustered, she started the other way, almost bumping into a man in soiled range clothes. He was long and angular and wolf-faced, with a great beak of a nose and wicked saffron eyes. He removed his black hat, showing a bald and shining dome.

"Look here at the little lady, Richie," he said in a deep, whimsical drawl. "Where are you-all bound to in a fine hurry, little lady?"

The man's face was ruddy with liquor, and the odor from his breath was sweetish. "Please," she said firmly. "You will let me pass."

"Aw no, now. Not till I have innerduced myself and friend. Jack Early of Nacogdoches, Texas, ma'am. Richie Sears here of, uh, where you from, Richie?"

His companion, standing to his left and a little behind him, was a desiccated wisp of a man whose wiry body indicated that he was younger than he looked. His face was a wry and shriveled mask, and the slack folds of his chin and his bright, half-lidded eyes gave him the appearance of a tired lizard. There was a trimness about his elaborately fringed trousers and embroidered jacket.

"I'm from most everywhere, Jack, but I know better'n you," Sears said quietly.

Early eyed him a fuddled moment. "Better'n what?"

"A Texan, drunk or sober, ought to know. Man don't fool with a decent woman, Jack."

The small man's meager speech was soft, but like the somber disillusionment in his bright eyes, somehow chilling. Thera did not like either of these men who wore their guns so handily, but she instinctively knew that of the two the smaller one was the more dangerous. A core of quiet viciousness underlaid his soft speech; he was simply a man who had nothing to prove and knew it.

Jack Early laughed and lifted a big-knuckled hand to touch her, saying, "Tell us your name, pretty." Another hand struck Early's aside before it reached her shoulder. Glancing around in surprise, Thera saw the lanky youth in the derby.

18

"Leave the young lady alone, you damned ruffian, or I will—" He grunted and staggered backward as Early backhanded him on the chest with a contemptuous rap.

"What you gonna do, dude," he murmured, "is back your big mouth. Or you be eatin' that funny hat."

Thera shuttled a frightened glance from one to the other, saying softly, "Please," but all three men ignored her. Richie Sears looked indifferent and faintly bored as he put his back to the building and tucked his thumbs in his belt.

A second cuff by Jack Early knocked the derby spinning into the street. The youth braced his feet apart, drawing himself erect. Thera's heart sank; he was quite drunk, and almost frail-looking beside Early. "That," said the youth, "was quite enough," and stepped in with his fists awkwardly cocked to swing wildly at Early's jutting jaw. His fist bounced lightly off the man's shoulder. Early's lips peeled away from his teeth; he smashed a long looping overhand into the youth's mouth. The young man gasped and dropped his hands. Early drove a leisurely fist into his middle, and he doubled and sank down retching.

Early took a fistful of his shirt and kept him upright and carried him backward into the alley between the store and the feed company. Pinning him to the wall, Early proceeded to work him over with carefully pulled punches.

Thera wheeled on the small man to cry that he stop it; his chill fish-lidded eyes changed her mind. She turned and hurried diagonally across the dusty street toward the newspaper building, holding her skirt high. "Papa." She let the word out in a shrill cry.

Almost at once Soderstrom exited from the building, coming to meet her in lunging strides. "Papa, help me—they are killing him!" Getting a shaky control on her voice then, she made an explanation.

Solderstrom gave only a stolid grunt. "That is not my lookout."

"Papa, don't you understand? He is getting killed because he tried to help me!"

Soderstrom's eyes swept the group of curious onlookers. His face wore a scowl which might have been mild embarrassment. He growled, "All right, all right," and almost before the words were out of his mouth Thera had seized his arm and was pulling him after her.

As they reached the alley, the youth was still upright, holding onto a dwindling consciousness, for Early was in no hurry, dragging it out almost scientifically.

"Here," grunted Soderstrom, "you," taking a long step into the alley as he spoke. Early turned his head, and Soderstrom's big fist met his shelving jaw like a cleaver hitting beef. Early spun about and fell on his face.

Instantly Richie Sears pushed away from the building. Thera's low warning word brought Soderstrom around to face the small man, his fist still lifted.

"You touch that gun, mister, and you will have a busted arm before you get it out." His voice matched his eyes, which were cold and ugly, and suddenly Thera, who had never feared her father, was afraid of him.

Richie Sears said, "Maybe you should back off now," in a whisper-dry voice.

He looked ready to fight, but now someone called from across the street, "You men slow down." Thera saw a man coming from a building with barred windows and SHERIFF black-lettered above the entrance. He was a tall old man with a gaunt, dour face beneath a smooth cap of dead-white hair. A star of office was pinned to the lapel of his neat well-worn suit. He came across the street with a stiff rheumatic stride.

Richie Sears said in his arid, toneless way, "Maybe we'll forget it." He stepped carefully around Soderstrom and gave a hand to Early who was pawing on his hands and knees. Supporting his groggy partner, Sears moved down the walk past the sheriff who did not even look at the two men. His mournful and faded eyes studied Soderstrom.

"You bought yourself a sack of hell, son, stirring up trouble in my town.".

Thera had taken vague notice of a young red-haired woman who had come up at the same moment the sheriff had. Before Soderstrom could answer, the red-haired lady said sharply, "You never forget who you're working for, do you, Otis?"

The sheriff eyed her mournfully. "You got a shrewish tongue in your head."

"Be that as it may, this man is a new county resident, land owner and taxpayer—he's bought Angus Horne's place—and anyway, Otis, I doubt he'll bully as easily as the average whiskeyed-up vagrant."

Ignoring her gibe, the sheriff said wearily, "You got any paper to show it?"

Soderstrom chewed his mustache and glowered, but Thera knew that he would not go against the law. He opened his coat and from an inner pocket withdrew a paper, unfolding it. The sheriff laboriously took out a pair of spectacles, set them on his nose, and pored over the paper with a testy care. Thera knew that it was perfectly valid, the property description being based on an exact government survey, and so turned her attention to the lank youth who was bracing himself against the wall, holding a soiled handkerchief to his bloody nose and mouth. His eyes were glazed with a residue of shock and liquor, and she said anxiously, "Please, you are all right?"

"Not—" His first word dissolved into a fit of terrible coughing, and when it had ebbed, he smiled feebly. "Not at all, Miss, but good of you. Very good."

The sheriff sighed and handed back the deed, then folded his spectacles and put them away. "You bought yourself a sack of hell."

The red-haired lady said with a hint of derision, "He's entitled to protection under the law if he needs it, Otis."

"I don't," Soderstrom overrode her words curtly. "I don't need trouble either, but any starting up will be finished by me. Just so that is understood."

The red-haired lady chuckled. "Don't worry, you can depend on Otis not to lift a finger on your behalf."

The old lawman gave her a look of weary disdain and then, moving with a stiff tired care, crossed back to his office. The lanky youth essayed an unsteady step away from the wall and nearly fell. Soderstrom caught him roughly by the arm. "Bring him over to the office," the red-haired lady suggested.

"He can clean up there." She gave Thera a friendly smile. "Are you with Mr. Soderstrom?"

"My daughter," Soderstrom said with what sounded like gruff reluctance. "Thera, this is Mrs. Kingery who owns the paper."

Thera breathed an "Oh" of fascination before remembering her father's very fixed ideas about a woman's place.

They crossed to the *Weekly Press* building, and Thera gazed about in wide-eyed wonder as Mrs. Kingery led them through the office and print shop to her quarters at the rear. These were a couple of simply furnished rooms with facilities for cooking and sleeping, and in small ways reflected a woman's touch as the brisk practicality of her office did not, Thera noticed.

The young man, who gave his name as David McIver of New York City, stripped off his coat and splashed water on his face. He seemed alert and clear-eyed then as he dried himself on a strip of worn towel, but Thera was still troubled by his thin, pale look. The frayed holes at the elbows of his sweater told of poverty; his sickly condition told of worse.

"Much better, ma'am. Thank you."

"Fine," said Mrs. Kingery. "Could you tell me what happened?"

Soderstrom frowned. "You mean to write this in a story?"

"Why not?" She gave him a level-eyed look. "Tell me, Mr. Soderstrom, is there anything of which you *do* approve?"

Thera said quickly, partly to forestall her father's temper, but also with an eager interest, "Oh, do you write?"

"I do everything," Mrs. Kingery said humorously. "Running a weekly paper is ordinarily a two-man job, but I'm only one woman. I have a nice modern treadle-press which is some help. Would you like to watch me set up a few lines of type?" She took Thera's arm as she led the way out to the typestand. "A very pretty name, Thera, but I'm afraid you'll have to tell me exactly how to spell it. Mine is Hannah, by the way. . . ."

Thera watched Hannah's typesetting skill with unconcealed awe, thinking, *She is wonderful! And how she stood up to Papa—I have never seen even a man do that for long.* Yet she was uncomfortably aware of her father's dark look. At least he gave civil responses as Hannah Kingery extracted the story from the three of them.

"There," she said, "all completed. If you'll come around later, you can see yourselves in print."

Soderstrom said, "We will be leaving town in a couple hours."

"Of course; you'll want to see your new place." She eyed him a speculative moment. "By the way, if the deed you showed Otis is the original, you'd better get it filed in the county records."

"You think somebody will try to steal it, missus?"

"If you're lucky, that's all that will happen," she said dryly as she slipped off the high stool. "I wouldn't guarantee the safety of your papers even in the county courthouse. Now you've met our sheriff, you may be inclined to agree."

"A foolish old man," Soderstrom grunted.

"That foolish old man is Otis Crashaw—a name that meant a good deal in the Kansas and Nebraska trail towns of twenty years ago. He was as fine a peace officer as the West has known."

"And now?"

"Now he's become an ineffectual relic coasting on his reputation in the comparative obscurity of a backwoods county, kowtowing to the powers that be. Mr. Soderstrom—perhaps you'll understand now. This town, this whole county, fits in my father's pocket with room to spare. Loftus Buckmaster built this country and built it to his taste. The Homestead Act, Pre-Emption Act, Timber Culture Act—he developed Wagontree by having his riders file land under all of them, then waiting out whatever time the law specified before they could sell and buy them out for a few dollars. And God help any man who crossed him."

Narrow-eyed, Soderstrom said, "But there were other homesteaders. And men like Angus Horne who bought up land and built good outfits for their own. He let them grow and stay, eh?"

"In those early days, yes. He wasn't nearly so big, and he was careful never to overextend himself. And some of them, like Mr. Horne, were friends of his. A few are still around.

But, as Angus may have told you, he and Pa had a falling-out and then Angus was cold turkey like the rest—the newcomers who've tried to homestead the remaining open range. He has held it so long, he can't conceive of letting it go. He's become, well, a fanatic." She smiled tiredly, tucking a straying wisp of red hair into place. "That is where I was foolish enough to think I had him where the hair is short. Pa had 'legally' deposed a number of government homesteaders by scaring them off before their prove-up time was ended. Twisting the big bad federal tail, so to speak. It was a good hook, so I wrote scathing articles on the terrorizing of government homesteaders and laxity of federal protection and ran off handbill-sized copies on my job press and sent them to every member of the U.S. Congress and every large newspaper in the country. Well, a minor rumble began in official circles, but I hadn't counted on Pa's influential friends in Washington—senators and lawyers who've prepared briefs on his behalf and now have the whole thing bogged down in red tape."

"Suppose a man owns his land and he stands on it with both feet planted solid. What can your pa do then?"

She shrugged lightly. "What did he do to Angus Horne? Anything short of outright murder, and usually it doesn't take much. How long anyone lasts depends on the quality of his nerves. I still have a mild suspicion that you are human, Mr. Soderstrom, and that no matter how tough you are you have nerves that can be worked on—that is how my father fights. Or rather hires men like Richie Sears to fight. If the law is bought off, what can you do? You sell out to my father at his price, if only to salvage something."

Thera's lively curiosity was greatly aroused, wondering why this remarkable woman should hate her father so; was it only his ruthlessness? But Ma, who had been a stickler for correct manners, had always warned her not to voice such thoughts.

Young David McIver gently cleared his throat. "I'll be on my way now. I want to thank—"

Thera had an inspiration; she said quickly, "Do you want work?"

McIver gave a bitter chuckle. "Want it? Miss, I've got to have work and soon."

"Papa, you need men—"

Soderstrom jerked out a dry laugh. "Him? You want me to hire this white-livered college boy?"

"He helped me and has been hurt for it. We should help him if we can." She gave a firm little nod. "That is only right."

"Girl, I'm too green myself to afford the hiring of greenhorn hands. I need men who know the work, able-bodied men." He tilted his head contemptuously. "Look at him. He drinks, too. No."

Hannah Kingery put in dryly, "Mr. Soderstrom, how many men can you name offhand who don't drink?"

Soderstrom turned his iron look on her, and Thera thought, *She knows already how he thinks and how to needle him; she enjoys it, too.* The interplay between them bemused Thera, and she said nothing now; it was McIver himself who spoke up defensively:

"About the drinking, I'll be honest. I'm consumptive. I came out from New York because my physician recommended a high, dry climate. I had barely enough funds to get this far, only to find myself unable to get a job of any sort. Your opinion, sir, is widely shared. Lately the spells have become so severe that I drink to kill the pain. If no liquor were available," he added quickly, "I could not very well drink. I would be willing to do any work assigned me for meals and board alone. And I can learn the work—everyone has to learn."

Soderstrom's regard was totally bleak; at last he said, "All right, college boy. You want to come on them terms you come. But by God, you will work, and anytime you slack off, out you go."

Thera touched her father's arm, smiling a little. Mrs. Kingery, as she accompanied them to the door, said pointedly, "Somehow I find it hard to believe that you have a grown daughter."

Soderstrom halted with a hand on the latch. "Why do you say this?"

"Certainly you had a wife."

"*Ja.*"

"That," Mrs. Kingery murmured, "is what I never would have suspected. You don't like women."

"Some women, maybe. There's something else you don't suspect."

"Oh, and what's that?"

"You have got ink on your chin. *Adjo,* missus."

Three

Before leaving town, Soderstrom had a last chore about which he took his time: the selection and purchase of a sturdy, well-seasoned spring wagon and a team of good horses. The proprietor of the livery barn had a number of rigs for rent or sale in back of his building, and Soderstrom ignored his spiel and made his round of the vehicles, studying each in turn.

A diffident voice spoke up behind him. "Mister?" Soderstrom turned, his bleak gaze settling on the hunched, scar-faced man he had seen in the newspaper office. He was holding a shovel and long-handled brush, and had evidently been swamping out the livery's stable.

"You seen me before. Waco Millard."

"*Ja,* I know. What do you want?"

Waco Millard took a hesitant step forward; his eyes were strangely bright. "I heard what you told Miss Hannah, that you aim to ranch under Buckmaster's nose. Didn't take much notice till I seen you put down that tough Jack Early. You ain't like these scared clodhoppers Buckmaster is pushed off. You'll make a fight, by God." His scarred face twitched. "Mister, hire me on. I don't want nothing but to side a man who'll take on Buckmaster."

Soderstrom was already shaking his head brusquely. "I have no use for you."

"You wouldn't never be sorry," Waco Millard said feverishly. "I was a top hand once and I know plenty. You need a man like that. You listen, mister."

"I don't need busted-up cripples," Soderstrom snapped. "They're no good to nobody." He pushed past the man, moving on to inspect another likely rig. Halting by it, he shot Millard a scowling look as the hunched swamper moved slowly back to the barn. There was something wrong in that man's head, he could swear; not all the damage was to his body.

Soderstrom found what he was looking for: a secondhand rig scarred with use but sound in every piece and joint. He called to the proprietor, who was chatting with Thera and McIver, and after many minutes of fierce dickering wore the price down to half the first offer.

Afterward they drove down to the general store where he picked up the heavy trunk he had left at the depot, loading it in the wagon bed. Then inside the store he checked over the articles Thera had purchased from his list. He had based his choice of gear and provisions on an outdoorsman's longtime experience—dried staple foods, cooking utensils, and blankets. Now he also carefully chose from the store's guncase a new Colt .45 and two secondhand Winchesters in good condition; he asked for ammunition, too.

With the supplies loaded, Thera beside him on the seat and McIver sitting awkwardly doubled in the wagon bed, Soderstrom took the reins and clucked up the team. Leaving town, he drove northeast onto the alkali flats as the scorching eye of the sun climbed against a dazzling blue. There was not a cloud in the sky, and already Soderstrom felt the suffocating pressure of the day's full heat. He began to sweat; he soon abandoned his coat and collar.

Following the directions given him by the livery owner, he took his bearings north-northeast by the loaf-shaped height of a black butte which tapered off toward a canyon-riddled valley. In many places the old road was almost obscured by wind-gusted dust, for Angus Horne had left his ranch a good eight months ago. He had discharged the last of his crew and left the Ladder shut down and deserted.

Squinting across the ridges dancing in the heat and the rim of distant gauzed peaks beyond, Soderstrom felt the dual discomforts of a northerner in a hot climate and a stranger in a new land coming to a home he hadn't seen.

Ah, what did you expect, Soderstrom? What did you think you were coming to—a little paradise, eh? No, that is not what you want; heaven is only for saints. But why did you come?

It might be only that all the old roots had gone bad; it might be no more than that. After Hedda had died, the meaning had gone out of his life. Then one bad year after another with his wheat farm; if it was not flattening hail, it was devouring locusts or a plunging market. It seemed that a man could not win, that he was besieged on all sides by enemies he could not touch. The relentless pressures on a man over many years came to fill his life, his whole outlook, with a bitter and brutal quality.

A need to shed bad memories or to make a new start or to satisfy a nameless, restless ache—what did it matter? A man who jarred himself in one deliberate move out of an ancient rut was not a man looking for the tame, the curried. This land of raw challenge could offer only abrasive new life or sudden death, and he welcomed the choice; he had been sparring with ghosts too long, and that was no good for a man.

They left the flats and moved across the broken valley through the heightening heat of forenoon, crossing rough talus slopes and crooked ridges. Past the valley, they mounted the slant of a shallow mesa bearded by a scrub growth of close-paced juniper and tangled mesquite. Here the old road made a plain and winding track through the timber. Soon it dipped into what he knew was the Salt Creek Valley and paralleled the creek itself, a meandering southward flow that had died to a shallow trickle in the blasting heat of late summer.

The surrounding valley was well-grassed, and time and time again they spooked up bunches of fat cattle branded and ear-marked Wagontree. This was his land, Soderstrom knew, and the sight of the alien cattle was fuel to his flint-edged mood.

He also saw a lone horseman on a not-distant hillock to the south, apparently following their progress across the valley. As Soderstrom watched, the man abruptly turned and vanished down the far slope. Something about the horsebacker and his action was disquieting; neither Thera nor McIver had taken notice of the rider and Soderstrom said nothing.

Presently the trail curved around a heavy shoulder of rock, and beyond this, snugged back within a deep fold formed by two granite hills and cut deeper by the roiling flow of the Salt Creek, was the Ladder layout. A few ratty cottonwoods shaded the rambling, one-storied adobe house. There was a 'dobe combination bunkhouse-cookshack, a frame barn and stable and outsheds, and a maze of pole corrals.

Soderstrom had seen enough ranch headquarters in Dakota to tell that the place had long ago become badly run-down, but then Angus Horne had not deceived him on that point. As he drove across the grassless barn lot toward the house, he noted the broken fences and the fouled corrals, and the stray pieces of old gear that had never been stored out of the weather.

Soderstrom halted the team in the cottonwood shade, came off the seat, and handed Thera down. McIver slipped to the ground on rubbery legs and was promptly doubled up by a coughing fit. Soderstrom shook his head with a dour disgust; he would be lucky to get the price of grub and a bunk out of this sick, ravaged college boy. But he had tried to help Thera, and this made a debt; also he would work wageless, a fact that almost balanced Soderstrom's need for experienced riders.

Sale of the farm had not brought a large sum, and as relatively small as Angus Horne's asking price had been, the buying of Ladder had left him desperately short on cash. Even the purchase of this wagon and team and a few supplies had eaten uncomfortably into his little reserve.

Moving up onto the sagging porch, he tried the latch. The door was wedged tightly; he kicked it twice before it creaked inward on rawhide hinges worn nearly through. He saw a rat scurry for cover in the gloom. Hazy sunlight streamed through cracks in the heavy wooden shutters, and old bullet scars pocking the adobe walls told of the days when the Apache marauders had held forth in the mountains to the west. The ancient hand-carved furniture, rough and serviceable token of Angus Horne's long tenure as a widower, was covered by thick dust which gave a mustiness to the air.

Each room, as they inspected it, was a study in disorder. The kitchen, which Horne had evidently made his all-purpose quarters, was the worst, bringing a choked little gasp from Thera. A Swedish girl absorbed a fetish for tidiness almost with her earliest understanding, and this lesson Thera had learned well from her immigrant mother. As she took in the floor and table littered with scraps of gear, magazines, and even dirty dishes and crusts of food, she bit her trembling underlip in consternation. But when she stepped into the room and her foot hit an empty bottle, an angry set came to her chin. "We will have to fix things up. We will start now."

Soderstrom grunted, stolidly kicking the wreckage of a broken chair from his path as he went to the shutters and threw them open. He turned to McIver. "There is a lean-to back of the place where grub is stored. Drive the wagon around there, then unhitch and water the team. Put them in the barn for now till we have got the fences fixed."

There was much to do, a fact grimly welcomed by Soderstrom as he discarded his wrinkled, sweaty suit trousers and boiled shirt in the room he had chosen for himself in the west wing. The afternoon sunlight streaming through the window gilded the bare mud-plastered walls; both bedrooms were innocent of furniture or fooferaw, except for a single narrow cot and moldy straw tick in the room that Thera had taken. He would have to throw his own blankets on the packed clay floor or bed down in the bunkhouse with McIver till he had constructed suitable beds and commodes. The slipshod condition that pervaded the whole place was what happened when a man's pride went out the window. A pride of a harsh and bitter sort that Krag Soderstrom had never lost.

He had questioned Angus Horne extensively, pored over cattleman's journals till his eyes ached; he still needed to familiarize himself with his own range and stock, but even that could wait. Until he had acquired an experienced hand or two for the actual work, there would be plenty of work just fixing up the place. He changed to thick-soled workshoes and well-worn duck pants and a fresh-bought workshirt whose prickly newness irritated his neck, retaining only his old slouch hat. He would break in his uncomfortable new half-boots when the time came.

Thera quickly whipped together a late midday meal of beans, biscuits, and coffee, and both Soderstroms ate with robust appetite. McIver could barely put down a few mouthfuls, though he drank a great deal of coffee. Soderstrom knew that the college boy was dying for a drink of whiskey—he had gone through a long bout with the bottle himself after Hedda died—but he felt no mercy for McIver. Either he would sweat out his craving or he would crack; there would be no halfway living on Krag Soderstrom's place.

The two men spent the afternoon carrying armloads of the useless trash that littered the house, bunkhouse, barn, and yard to a bonfire that Soderstrom set on a bare spot off back of the barn. Meantime Thera was everywhere at once, briskly directing the whole operation; she carried dozens of things outside to air out in the sunlight; she found a bar of strong yellow soap from which she pared shavings into a pail of water and set to scrubbing down the kitchen, the bedrooms and part of the bunkhouse "so we will all sleep good tonight." Only then would she permit the food and utensils, blankets and belongings, to be brought inside.

She, with her high spirits and quiet laughter, made a game of the work; Soderstrom, driving himself with a dogged grimness, several times caught her talking and laughing with McIver and was not pleased. They were too young to take things seriously enough, and while McIver seemed a decent sort, he did not fancy Thera taking to a sick college boy; somehow it did not seem right.

Muttering and chewing the tips of his mustaches, Soderstrom gathered up the two empty water buckets in the kitchen and tramped out past the barn and the trash fire, swinging up the creek where it meandered past the outbuildings. Angus Horne had said that the well was off back of the place. He found it above the brushy creek-bank, and it boasted plenty of clear water.

As he dipped the first bucket full, Soderstrom made out a sound of horses coming from downcreek. Setting down the bucket, he headed back along the bank, keeping the barn between himself and the house. He heard a man's voice, loud and strident, and had a moment of regret that he had not strapped on his new Colt. But he had left a rifle leaning by the barn wall against emergency, and now as he picked it up, feeling the good familiarity of stock and barrel, he felt better. He had been a hunter all his life, and this was his kind of weapon.

He flattened himself along the wall by the corner, exposing his head enough to pick out the five men sitting their horses in the front yard. Among them he identified the two with whom he had clashed in town—Thera had caught their names as Early and Sears—which meant that these were Wagontree men. All five were armed to the teeth, and Soderstrom did not wait to see more.

Wheeling about, he moved along the barn wall till he achieved the brush that rimmed one of the flanking hills. He made his way with noiseless care along the base of the hill, keeping always behind the wall of shrubbery, and emerged from it well downcreek; he came to the cover of the rocky shoulder where the road turned into the place. Stepping around the shoulder now, as he brought up his rifle, he was not sixty feet behind the horsemen.

Both McIver and Thera, who had been in the house, were now in the yard facing the men. One, a huge and thick-bodied fellow who had reined out ahead of the others, said, "All right, so your pa is the boss. Where is he?"

Thera spoke quietly and shook her head, and the huge man turned his prancing black on a rough rein and spoke to the others, "Spread out and find him then."

Soderstrom levered the Winchester and said in a tight and ugly way, "No. You stay all together. Keep your hands in sight." He saw Sears and Early exchange glances as they recognized him. The other two hands, a slim mustachioed fellow and a heavy-set blond youth, appeared to be of a common stripe—gun-hung, dangerous men.

The leader paced his black around the others to get a clear look at Soderstrom. A muscled mountain of a man in the dust-soiled dignity of a black suit, he was massive in every part of his body. Kidskin gloves sheathed the hamlike fists knotted around his lifted reins. His black-bearded face was heavily fleshed, filled with bluff arrogance; his low black nests of eyebrows made a perpetual scowl. He was in his mid-thirties, which meant that he was not Loftus Buckmaster, whom Angus Horne had described as a white-haired giant. One of the sons, Soderstrom guessed.

"Your name is Buckmaster?"

"Garth Buckmaster."

"I will give you maybe ten seconds to say what you want," Soderstrom said in a quiet tone of iron. "Then you will ride. I know you, and I tell you don't waste my time. I have bought the deed on this place, and I am here to stay."

The huge man rumbled his laughter. "That don't matter, fella. Horne had paper on this outfit and he couldn't hold it. Neither will you."

Soderstrom was not impressed. Garth Buckmaster's habit of authority sat him like a heavy fist, but whatever directed the fist was not here. "You figured you would show us that now," Soderstrom said softly. "Riding straight in with four armed men at your back. You have had it easy, pushing around people who are scared, eh? You did not figure on a man who is ready for you. Maybe here is something else you did not figure on."

Deliberately he swung the rifle level, and Buckmaster smiled, "You won't use—" The crash of the rifle shattered the warm stillness; the black reared with a squeal of pain, rump-seared. The big man pitched from his saddle, and the impact of his fall shook the ground. He rolled heavily to his hands and knees, then scrubbed a gloved hand over his face. Soderstrom saw the sudden furtive fear in his eyes and felt a long-delayed pleasure; a wolfish grin bared his teeth.

"So. You are trespassers, and a man can shoot his trespassers."

"You don't want to kill a man for—"

"I want to," Soderstrom murmured. "You don't know me yet, mister. Now you find out. Get off your horses. I hit the horse where I shot at him; think of this before you try anything."

The four men still mounted made a cautious dismount and then, at Soderstrom's curt order, let their shell belts and pistols drop. He was about to tell them to remove their boots, when it occurred to him that this tight vain cowman's footgear was not made for walking.

"I will turn your horses loose tomorrow," he said, and pointed his rifle sideways at the ground. "The guns you can come get sometime, if you dare. Now. There is the road."

The small man called Sears spat quietly at the ground; his eyes were like coals in his lined and wattled face, and there was no fear in him. He walked straight ahead, not even looking at Soderstrom as he tramped a bare yard away from him. The others shuffled forward. Buckmaster got to his feet and beat his hat uncertainly against his pants, then followed his men. The four filed around Soderstrom at a tense, careful distance.

"Papa," Thera called hesitantly. "Maybe this is not—"

Soderstrom rapped out harshly, "Be still," and watched the five men as they struck south across the rolling grass. He had settled nothing, he knew grimly. But for Thera's presence, he would have shot them up some at least. He was not sure, but he thought it might even be easy to kill such men.

Four

Soderstrom kept working steadily until well after dark. He and McIver were repairing a broken section of corral by lanternlight when Thera called them to supper. By now the college boy was exhausted; he literally collapsed into his chair. Probably, Soderstrom thought grimly, he had not put in such a day in his soft citified life. Actually this had been only a half-day; tomorrow and the tomorrows to follow would be far more grueling. A healthy man could have done the same work in half the time—still, McIver came free. And he would lose his softness or die trying. *No, not that,* Soderstrom amended contemptuously. *Not the college boy; he will quit first.* But he was no longer so sure, grudgingly having to concede that McIver threw himself into whatever he did without a grimace of complaint.

Thera bustled back and forth between stove and table, laying out a savory meal of bacon, hot smoking cornbread, and good coffee as her father liked it, black and strong. "David," she rebuked, "you do not eat like you mean it. My cooking is so bad?"

"No," the youth said with a lame haste. "All very good, I'm sure, but I may be a while getting back my appetite."

Soderstrom gave him a small cold grin. "The drinking, eh?"

"Partly." McIver flushed slightly, but resentment tinged his voice. "Sickness can also contribute, or so I've been told."

Thera said with her firm and sunny faith, "Soon you will eat good," and moved briskly back to the stove. She opened the oven, lifted out a canned-apple pie and carried it to the table; she sat down to eat and chatted lightly with McIver, refusing to look at her father. She had not spoken directly to him since he had harshly silenced her this afternoon.

Soderstrom was troubled. No matter how gruff his moods, he had hardly ever raised an angry word to Thera.

Her fair skin was still pinkened by stoveheat as she began to clear the table. Watching her brisk young grace, the reflection in her face of a liveliness that never seemed to touch the grave gray eyes, Krag Soderstrom felt a deep and sudden pang. How like Hedda she was ... and not a day younger than Hedda on that day some eighteen years ago when a fresh-faced immigrant girl hardly two weeks out of a ship's steerage, less than two months from her native Sweden, had come as hired girl to the midwest farm where he was working and saving wages for a place of his own. Within the week she was his bride, and in the ten years they had had together he had not regretted once that fast, impulsive courtship. His bride—so quick, so young, so suddenly cold in her grave. Again the pang, cutting as a knife, swiftly smothered with iron gruffness. The sad ache hardly lessened with each passing year, and he wished that it would; for it made intolerable the many good memories he would have liked to relive. Yet oddly now, one memory did bring a lightness that relaxed his mouth under the drooping mustache. For Thera was censuring his harshness in exactly her mother's old manner: he was nothing, he did not exist, till she should choose to notice him again.

"Go to bed," he told McIver. "It will be dark yet when we are up tomorrow." Rising, Soderstrom passed through the house and stepped out onto the sagging front veranda. An autumn chill touched the early evening. He took out his tobacco pouch and stubby blackened pipe, absently filling it as he swung his gaze around the dark layout. He could not see much, but his mind's eye was busily reconstructing the run-down outbuildings and broken fences; this would again be a good place. Impatience threaded his thoughts; tiredness laid only a slight drag on his muscles. Tomorrow they would ache a little, and then he would be back in the zesty swing of living and working; to Krag Soderstrom there was little difference any more.

A horse, probably one of the restless Wagontree ponies, nickered faintly in the barn. He struck a match and cupped the flare to his pipebowl; his lips were set around the stem or he would have grinned. Those men had expected an easy mark; they would be back. Perhaps with others. Soderstrom took the pipe from his mouth to let the grin form; he did not mind the odds being tough and big. But his lips sobered; there was Thera to consider. And the college boy too since he could not fight. Maybe he could shoot a little, though Soderstrom dourly doubted it. That was a qualification he should have specified in his ad. But remembering Hannah Kingery's words about the riders hereabouts being skittish of her father, he thought, *No matter, they will know*. As he would soon enough know whether the ad produced results.

A curious turn veered his thought wholly to Hannah Kingery. She was a strange sugar-with-spice sort of young woman, flippant and tart-tongued and gentle by turns, and with a well of hidden reserve that he sharply sensed without knowing why. She was clever and several-sided, which tended to discourage any judgment he might make; if asked he would say he did not like her, but privately he was sure only that he disapproved of her. His idle musings carried him from the thought that, clever or not, she was probably useless in a kitchen, to a mild wonderment that such a woman could be the sister of a thick-headed brute like the Buckmaster he had met this afternoon. But maybe someone who knew Thera and himself would be as greatly surprised.

Soderstrom shook himself, irritated at this thinking. He knocked out his pipe against a veranda post, then turned to enter the house. As he opened the door, a bullet hammered into the jamb inches from his left shoulder.

Not sparing even an instant to glance backward, he lunged through the doorway as the shot echoes rattled between the granite hills. Soderstrom slammed the door, shot the boltlock, and wheeled for the wall to snuff the lamp; he detoured slightly to snatch up his rifle.

Even as the room ebbed into darkness a fusillade of rifle shots opened in concert from the embracing hills. Bending low, Soderstrom moved from window to window, securing the shutters of each while a steady hail of slugs pattered the outside walls. He heard quick steps as his daughter and

McIver entered the parlor, their voices excited; he barked, "Thera!"

After a moment she said calmly, "Here, Papa," from over by the first shuttered window. There he caught a gleam of steel where moonlight streamed through the shooting port that perforated a shutter and that was usually covered by a hinged block of wood. Soderstrom uttered a quiet oath. He knocked over a chair getting to her and roughly took the second rifle from her. "Down! Stay down on the floor, I tell you. McIver, this gun, take it and shoot. Shoot at the flashes. A bad shot or good, in the dark and at this range, it makes no difference."

When he felt McIver's hand close on the gun, he returned to the last window he had secured and took his position at the port. He opened up with a steady drumming fire at the stabs of gunflame high on the slopes. As he had told McIver, there was little hope of hitting anything when your only targets were elusive powder-flashes.

So this was Wagontree's retribution. He did not know whether they meant to kill or only frighten, but that first bullet had been dangerously near. The thick shutters absorbed the hail of lead so efficiently that no more bullets found their way inside; but the advantage still lay with the enemy. The random sprinkling of gunflashes showed them scattered widely in a straggling line about two-thirds of the way upslope; also, the shifting pattern of shots showed the riflemen to be always changing position, offering no constant target. Meantime they had only to direct a steady fire on the stationary fire from the two shooting ports.

Now, as Soderstrom had feared, they were getting the range, difficult in downhill shooting. As he pulled back from the port to refill his magazine, a whistling slug found the aperture and caromed off the inside walls.

At the other port McIver was keeping up an even, competent fire. Obviously he was no stranger to a rifle, and he did not shrink from danger: even in this chaotic moment these facts left a strong impression on Krag Soderstrom.

"Sir, I will need more cartridges."

"You need nothing," Soderstrom growled, "but to get down on the floor and stay there. Do it now."

"But—"

"Do as I say and get your fool head down or lose it. They are finding the range and bullets don't bounce off these holes. Get down!" As he spoke Soderstrom crossed the room intending to hurry through the house to the rear. He'd had the cold thought that probably this frontal assault was a diversion; there were three more sides to the house, all undefended. He would secure all shutters and bar the back door.

Then McIver's excited voice brought him to a stop. "Sir, look. Something's happened out there. Someone on top of the hill seems to be shooting. Can't be sure, but I think it's at them—"

"Eh?" Soderstrom returned to his port, squinting at the black loaf of the hill. The boy was right. An isolated gun was speaking from the topmost height, and the ragged pocks of gunfire below were disappearing. A confused outbreak of voices drifted off the dark slope, and now it was plain: the Wagontree men were pulling out. There was, shortly, a muted clatter of hooves as the whole body of riders headed away upvalley.

At last Thera broke the trailing silence. "There is a friend out there. Papa, we—"

"Be still. Maybe this is a trick."

Soderstrom moved back to the port and placed his eye to the opening, watching the moonlit yard. After a long while he saw a man's lanky form detach itself from the black shape of the hill and start across the yard. Soderstrom levered his Winchester, the noise carrying with a metallic sharpness.

The man out in the night halted beyond a fence. "Halloo, the house."

"Who are you?"

"Man looking for a bait and a bunk."

"You got a rifle," Soderstrom called.

"Sure I got a rifle. I used it on them yahoos shooting at you."

"What I mean, you put down the rifle before you come on. I

can see you good, mister. Keep the hands away from your body."

Soderstrom watched until assured that his directions were being followed; he stepped back to the table and struck a match. Again the soft lamprays spread through the room. He saw with some anger that McIver had stayed at his window, and worse, that Thera had quietly taken her post at the unoccupied port. She had the Colt .45, holding it ready, though she disliked guns and could not have hit a bull broadside even with a rifle.

Wordlessly Soderstrom took her by the shoulders and propelled her firmly to a chair, then stepped to the doorway. He eased back the bolt and nudged open the door with a foot, then cut sideways behind it. Steps sounded on the veranda. As the man stepped inside, blinking against the light, Soderstrom closed the door and in doing so moved behind him.

The man whirled. "Mister, don't ever come behind a man that way."

Soderstrom roughly nudged his belly with the Winchester, edging him backward. "You do not give the orders. Move ahead of me. Move!"

They entered the kitchen, where Soderstrom turned up the lamp. The newcomer's blinking, temper-worn glance touched each of them in turn. He was about thirty and narrow as a lath, with a pugnacious, long-jawed face. His hair was red and unruly and untrimmed under his horse-thief hat, and the lamplight gilded a week's growth of fiery whiskers. His faded denims were soft with age and use, worn almost chalky at the knees and elbows. There was a feel of something untamed and free-ranging about him that, in a less prickly moment, might be oddly engaging.

"Sit down," Soderstrom said coldly. The man straddled the bench and folded his scarred hands on the table, tight-lipped.

"Why do you come here, mister?"

"Can I move my hand?"

"So you keep it in sight."

The man reached for a folded newspaper protruding from

his jacket pocket, and unfolded it on the table. "If that's your ad in the corner, I'm answering it."

Soderstrom's bleak gaze did not change. "Now tell what happened out there."

The rider's bony shoulders faintly stirred. "That ain't much of a say. I was coming on the road and seen a passel of men riding up from the south. I pulled off the road and waited—"

"Why?"

"Because I knew why they was here. Hell, anybody in the county who knows there's a new owner on Ladder could tell that. I saw 'em leave their horses and take to the high ground, and lay up there. When it was clear what they was about, I tied my horse and came up the other side of the hill. I got above them and shot down. I nicked one for sure, and hit or scared another from his bellowing. Then they cleared out."

"Why do you come looking for a job this time of night?"

"Because I live way back in the hills and got into town late today and didn't see a paper till then. I decided right off and saw no sense waiting." The man placed his palms on the table and half-rose, slightly bristling. "I don't fancy hard-nose questions off a man I pulled out of a jackpot. I had better receiving than this from folks don't owe me a thing."

"Sit down," Soderstrom said quietly. "There is another question. Can you work cows?"

"Yes, by God, man and boy."

"Thera, bring food. Your name, mister?"

"Rafe Catron."

"If you have your own blankets, there is a place in the bunkhouse."

The rider sank back on the bench and stared dourly at the table. Soderstrom briefly introduced himself and his daughter and McIver as Thera set a loaded plate and a cup of steaming coffee in front of the stranger. He attacked the food with a fury that indicated most of his days were lean ones. Soderstrom sensed that only a rawhide pride provoked the man's refusal when Thera offered seconds; he let his coffee cup be freshened. Then he picked up his hat and rose. "Obliged. I left my horse back of the hill. I'll see to him and throw my stuff in your bunkhouse."

Soderstrom told him to come to the house afterward. Catron nodded and went out; and Soderstrom inspected the newspaper he had brought. It featured an editorial blistering Hannah Kingery's father; she might have been writing about a stranger.

Rafe Catron returned, accepted a third cup of coffee, and got a cigarette going. Soderstrom said then: "I am told, mister, I would have it hard getting riders. About the time I am thinking all I can get is maybe college boys, you come. All right. You say you know cow work. And you don't look stove-up anyway I can guess."

"I ain't."

"Then why you this out at the heels, eh?"

Catron looked ready to bristle again, but then as if in concession that the contradictions about him deserved explanation, he grunted, "Never liked working for another man. Never stick long. Plenty times I've said I'd sooner starve by my lonesome than take another man's guff, and plenty times I came close to it." He paused, then added grudgingly, "That is part of it. Maybe you should know the rest."

"If there is more, you tell it."

"You always this hard-nosed?"

"That is right," Soderstrom said flatly.

"I got a place back in the hills," Catron snapped. "It ain't much. I make do by hunting, trapping, wolfing for bounty. I raise a few goats and a little truck. Once in a while I come down to the valley and work cows a spell.

"Last year I was doing some spring branding for Henderson, a one-loop rancher over east of here. Was out in the brush by myself and about to draw a straight iron on a new calf when some Wagontree riders showed up. Both Buckmaster boys, Garth and Chad, was with 'em. There is a dim view of mavericking hereabouts, and we had words. Then the Wagontree crowd hazed over the cow which was nearby and clipped the winter hair off her brand. It was Wagontree, sure enough. They called it rustling. I called it a mistake. Said I was working for Tom Henderson, and was about to put on his brand. Hell, I ran a few head some years back and I got a brand registered in the county book. Everyone knows that.

Garth Buckmaster said it was time they showed a lot of long-looping poor trash the what-for of things.

"I said it wouldn't take an hour to check with Tom Henderson. He would bear me out. Chad said that sounded all right. He is the sly one of the two and a heap more careful. Garth is all beef and cussedness, but is the oldest and has got the say-so for his pa. So he give the word and they strung me up and rode away. I was kicking away black in the face when this tree branch busted and dumped me down. It was an hour before I could get about. Then I made it home and laid up for a week."

Catron tipped up his pugnacious chin and exposed his throat. The long rope-scar made a raddled shine under the light. "When I was up and about I done nothing for a month but practice with my guns, rifle and handguns. I had had luck trapping, and every cent has gone for shells. I been ready for anything, but I ain't made a fight. No lonesome man can make a fight. I come across your ad, so thought I would have a look at you."

"Well," Soderstrom said grimly, "you seen me."

"I see you, and mostly I wouldn't put up with your hard-nosed sort in a year of Sundays." Catron's ruddily weathered face darkened. "But you'll fight."

"You think so?"

"They'll bring the fight to you and you won't back off. That's clear as day." Catron lounged to his feet, a deep satisfaction in his tough face. "I'd work a job for beans and biscuits for a chance like this."

"You think there'll be more hoorawing like tonight, eh?"

"Not much." Catron chuckled "They will think that was one of you shooting from above 'em tonight. They'll think you outsmarted 'em and put someone up there. That will make 'em take a long second look, and next time they will come for keeps. They have been pushing folks off by playin' pat-a-cake so long they may be slow about toughing up. But you wait."

"Tomorrow," Soderstrom said, "we will start working cattle."

Catron gave a bare nod that included them all and tramped out the back door. McIver said good night, and doubled up in a coughing fit as he went out. Thera went to the doorway and called after him, "David, keep warm tonight. Make a good fire in the stove." She closed the door and leaned her back to it momentarily, her face softened by lamplight and hidden thoughts.

Soderstrom made a gruff sound in his chest as he stood, fumbling with his dead pipe. "I did not mean to shout at you."

She laughed, "Heavens, I had forgot," but her brief-touching glance irritated him. Maybe it was not pity in her face just then. But something uncomfortably close to it.

Five

Rafe Catron moved his few belongings from his deep-hill place to Ladder. After he had helped Soderstrom with the selection and buying of some good horseflesh, the bitter business of hazing the scrawny, half-wild steers out of the eastern foothill country began. It was a region studded with steep-pitched ridges, mazed by abrupt coulees, and choked with tangled thickets. Catron said that after Angus Horne had abandoned Ladder, the Wagontree riders had pushed much of the Ladder beef back into this barren, broken country, fit only for scanty browsing. Meantime their own cattle had been quietly drifted onto the long rolling slopes and grass flats. At Catron's advice, Soderstrom did not now waste time chousing off these trespassing beefs except when they chanced on good-sized bunches; these would be driven back toward Wagontree at a tallow-shedding pace.

On the first day Thera aroused her father's genuine wrath when she appeared wearing an outfit she had bought the day before unbeknown to him: a man's shirt and trousers, as well as a panama hat and cowman's half-boots, all somewhat oversize.

"I will not have you showing yourself about in man's clothes," Soderstrom roared.

"Papa, with only two men, you will need me. Till David is better I will help."

That settled the matter, Soderstrom finding some release for his seething temper by blaming young McIver. He saw to it that McIver rode the meanest trails, ate more than his share of dust, and handled the most grueling chores. McIver took the full brunt of his savage cussings which, when Thera was not nearby, were pungent and frequent.

Day after day the steady grind continued. Where the rugged terrain was not boxed by sheer sandstone walls or treacherous slides, it was masked by a rioting overgrowth. Daily they broke trail through canyons choked by catclaw and yucca to herd out handfuls of rib-lean steers that had penetrated the cruel cover to slake their thirst at some isolated sink containing a few inches of slime-covered water. They were in pathetic condition, but once moved to the good lower grasses they would add poundage quickly, Catron said.

Soderstrom dourly hoped so, for he was fighting time. He was nearly flat broke, and he could not look for credit in a town where the guiding hand was Loftus Buckmaster's. His only hope of lasting out this year was to fatten enough beefs for an early trail drive to a railhead market while the stock prices held high.

For all of them the first two weeks were a nadir of nightmarish exhaustion. It was stagger out of your blankets in the murky pre-dawn and enter a world composed of dust and sweat and broiling heat, the creak of leather, the sting and tear of brushy barbs, the crackle of branding fires, the bawling of cattle, and the stench of burning hair and flesh. Always the dull ache of a deadly mechanical routine where one frustrating day melted into the next. You came not to notice the rankness of your clothes ingrained with dirt and old sweat. At day's end you sought your blankets and a gray dreamless stupor. And rolled out before dawn to begin the savage circle all over again.

Thera's fair skin burned badly, and she suffered with the heat. She was a sturdy girl, but still this was a man's work whose demands she could not meet. She did her best, with a fortitude and good cheer that was incredible. Even Soderstrom, driving himself harder than any of them if only because even if they had their limits he would admit none, shed every ounce of excess tallow and was dehydrated to clean sinew and muscle. The same with Rafe Catron, who admitted he'd tackled no such job as this in his life. The indifferent currents of his existence hadn't before been so doggedly channeled toward the goals of a Krag Soderstrom.

But it was McIver who suffered the most. His soft hands blistered till even rein-guiding a horse was an agony. His sallow face, where a dirty beard did not obscure it, burned beet-red and peeled and burned again. His slender frame was pared to bony angles, and he tottered about like a gaunt, hollow-eyed ghost. Long after the want of drink ceased to burn like a fever in his cheeks, his coughing fits worsened; he ate little and his stomach retained less. Twice he passed out on particularly tough chores and had to be packed back to headquarters. At these times only Thera's intercession prevented her father from carrying out his promise and discharging him outright.

"You are goddamn lucky, college boy," Soderstrom would rumble darkly, and was always there to goad him whenever McIver began to slip with sickness and exhaustion. "I found a bottle of whiskey old man Horne left on the place, college boy. You want me to tell you where it is, eh? Maybe that would give you some belly."

Even the taciturn Rafe Catron was moved to some spare words in McIver's defense: "You ought to leave Mac alone, Mr. Soderstrom. The boy has got guts to stick on, sick as he is." Soderstrom's reply was not fit for Thera's ears, but he began to let up on McIver all the same. The boy's sheer tenacity provoked his respect, and he could only surlily guess at why he would not knuckle under. Certainly McIver must hate him; maybe it was that acid spur of fury that drove him on. Or maybe it was mostly Thera, with the words or smiles that were a sunny extension of her whole spirit: "You did better today, David; tomorrow you will do better yet. You will see."

And McIver's rock-bottom misery did lessen a little. His appetite got better; his color improved somewhat and his coughing fits were less severe, partly perhaps because Soderstrom abandoned his savage pressures on the boy entirely as he came to the realization that the more he hazed McIver, the more Thera stubbornly took his part. She was coming to like him too much, and you could never tell about a slick-tongued college boy. Although had Soderstrom been asked to explain from his knowledge of McIver's character exactly why he took a bitter exception to him, he couldn't have done so.

As the work went on, Soderstrom kept an iron alert against trouble. He saw that nobody's duty took them out of hailing distance of the others. More than once they spotted distant riders watching from open heights of land, which meant that Wagontree was keeping a watchful eye on their progress. And would not let this threat to their habitual authority go unchallenged. But when and how would they strike?

The day came when Catron gave it as his opinion that the bulk of Soderstrom's scrub stock had been combed out of the breaks. At supper that night Soderstrom announced his intention of starting a gather of as many now-fattened cattle as they could handle for a drive. Thera then made the practical observation that their food supply was low and decided in the same breath that McIver would accompany her to Mimbreno. Soderstrom did not object, partly because her tone settled the matter, partly because it would be improper for a young girl to go alone to town, though he put his assent typically: "He might as well go along with you, girl, for all he gets done around here."

Next day, while a drowsing coolness still clung to the morning, McIver stiffly took his place on the seat of the spring wagon beside Thera. Soderstrom frowningly checked the harness and regretfully found that the college boy had hitched up properly.

Thera gave her father a happy smile as he looked up from a headstall. She made a picture of unbelievable freshness and radiance in her crisp fresh calico, bell-skirted and fitted gently to her upper body. She was a bit thinner now, and her last sunburn, a mild one, had peeled to a golden tan. Her starched bonnet lay in her lap; the sun made a pale blaze of the heavy braid wrapped like a gleaming coronet around her head. A catch of memory stung Soderstrom's throat; he scowled at McIver. "You keep your nose clean, mister, you hear?"

That could mean almost anything, and McIver's lobster-burned face colored a faint shade deeper. He tilted his battered derby to a mildly defiant angle and clucked up the team. Soderstrom stood watching them wheel down the road. Then he briskly went to the corral where Catron had their ponies saddled.

The two men spent the day selecting and driving jags of the fattest steers to a large box canyon, confining them inside with a pair of maguey ropes stretched across the mouth. Catron thought they could start driving north to Taskerville in three days. At sunset they returned dog-tired to headquarters and threw together a supper of bacon and warmed-up beans and cold biscuits. McIver and Thera had not returned, and Soderstrom gruffly confessed to some concern.

"Hell," Catron said, holding a sputtering lucifer to his after-supper cigarette. "You know for a couple of kids going to town is like a pardon from stony lonesome. No cause to worry."

Soderstrom grunted as he packed his pipe; he went to the fireplace and puffed the tobacco alight from a flaming twig, eyeing Catron's back through the smoke. Rafe was a hard worker who had brought a needed know-how to the job; yet Soderstrom mistrusted the current of hidden tension he felt in the man. Catron had been aboveboard in stating his reason for hiring on: to strike at Wagontree and the Buckmasters when the chance came. But still Soderstrom was not quite sure of him, and he did not know why.

He stepped out on the porch; his pipesmoke made a frosty ribbon on the nipping, still air. He let his glance circle with satisfaction the headquarters area in the lowering dusk. The litter of trash had been cleaned up; a broken fence boasted freshly peeled rails; the warped and sagging door on the tack shed was replaced, these and other improvements having been made in what odd moments could be found after a day's work.

A restless irritation touched him so that he was about to saddle up and learn what had delayed McIver and Thera. Then he heard the wagon approaching on the road. Frowning, he knocked out his pipe and grimly considered the blistering what-for he would give them. He did not, in the growing darkness, make out the two people until the wagon rolled into the outspill of window light. Then he saw that the man beside Thera on the seat was not McIver; it was the hunched old cripple called Waco Millard who had wasted his time asking to hire on .

Thera was already scrambling to the ground as Waco halted the team; she ran into her father's arms, and she was trembling wildly. "Here, girl," he growled. "Stop shaking and say what this is about."

"Papa, oh papa, he is hurt so bad! Get the doctor please!" She caught his arm and drew him to the wagon bed. Here McIver lay on his back between the stacked supplies, and Soderstrom roared for Catron to bring out the lamp.

McIver's face, in the sickly light, was almost unrecognizable. His clothes were torn to shreds; his whole body was savagely lacerated. His breath was a bubbling rasp through his broken nose.

Soderstrom let the picture etch with a raw bleakness into his mind and said quietly, "We get him inside, Catron. Give Thera the lamp. Now mind you lift careful so we don't mash a lot of bones."

Six

When they had gotten McIver into Soderstrom's own room and applied carbolic to the worst of his hurts, Soderstrom asked the brittle question. It was Waco Millard, hovering by the doorway like a bird of bad omen, who croaked up at once, "It was a Dutch ride. He got dragged on a rope."

Soderstrom darted him an agate-hard stare, then looked at his daughter. "Tell it all, girl. Leave out nothing."

As Thera told the story she did not take her eyes off the boy's mangled face.

After they had done the shopping in town and had loaded the wagon, she had gone to the newspaper office to chat with Hannah Kingery while McIver went to a saloon for a drink. There he had encountered four of the men from Wagontree, two of them Jack Early and Richie Sears. Early had wanted to take up the quarrel from weeks before when he had beat McIver with his fists, and so he had pushed David to a fight.

"Then dragged him behind a horse," Rafe Catron said bitterly. "What was that damned sheriff doing?"

No, Thera said impatiently, that was not how it was. McIver had met the drunken, blustering Early out on the street and shot him down. Then—

"Mac done for Early?" Catron could not believe it. "But he don't even pack a gun."

Waco Millard cackled softly. "I give him mine." And tugged a rusty old pistol from his belt and held it up. "I was swamping in the place when Early called him out. Early said he had better have a gun in five minutes because he would come smoking then whether he did or not. He was powerful drunk, Early was. McIver was pretty pale but was bound to defend his honor, he says, so I fetched him this old gun hid in my poke. Told him to aim like he was pointing a finger and take his time. Hell, Early had a slip gun; he come at this boy fanning bullets like he was spraying ladies' coloney, and by God, this Mac took aim and shot once and busted him wide open."

Catron whistled quietly, and Soderstrom motioned for his daughter to go on.

Then, she said, the sheriff had been ready to jail McIver. Surprisingly, it had been Early's friend Richie Sears who had laconically enjoined Sheriff Crashaw to let McIver go his way, as the case was one of clear-cut self-defense. Sears and the other two Wagontree hands had taken Early to the undertaking parlor, and then promptly left town.

Thera had been afraid as they drove home toward Ladder, remembering the look on Sears' face. They had been alert for trouble during the ride, not relaxing until they were well past the turnoff to Wagontree headquarters and within a couple of miles of home. Then, as they rode around an abutting shoulder, Sears and the pair of toughs were waiting.

Thera shuddered; she would never forget the small man's words or the tone of them. *Jack Early had a big mouth and he was a fool. Still he was the only partner I ever had, boy. I ain't about to do for you; old Buckmaster don't want killing. Maybe you will wish you was dead. . . .*

Soderstrom shook her insistently by the shoulders. "The man who dragged him, this was Sears, eh? Thera?"

"Yes, yes, but please get a doctor now, papa. We were so close to home I brought him on here, but now he must have a doctor."

"I'll go," Rafe said, and tramped out.

Soderstrom stood by the window as Catron's horse drummed away on the road. *They will pay for this night's work,* he thought with a massive certainty, and finally settled his frosty stare on Waco Millard. "What does he do here?"

"Why, if he had not given David the gun, that Early would have shot David down. And then he asked if maybe now you would hire him. So I told him to come along, and papa, please do not tell him no."

"Give a man a chance, mister," husked Waco Millard. "I

will do anything you set me to." His scarred face twitched. "I will work for 'most nothing."

"All right, you have got a chance coming. I need another man for the trail drive. But you will put in a whole man's work. You pull your freight or out you go."

Rafe returned with Dr. Enever, a sandy-haired young man with conspicuous jaundice and a temper. He made his examination and said that McIver appeared internally sound except for a dislocated arm which he had set. The damage to his slashed and welted face, bad as it looked, was superficial; he put a bandage on the nose. What the boy needed now was rest and care. Once McIver came to long enough to whisper through puffy lips, "Working for you can be rather a harrowing adventure, Mr. Soderstrom."

Soderstrom was impatient to deal with Richie Sears; he meant to go to Wagontree headquarters and keep a watch on the place as long as necessary to catch Sears alone. He would need Rafe Catron's knowledge of the country to help form his strategy. But Catron said, "Let's don't go off half-cocked, Mr. Soderstrom. Wagontree is a hell of a big outfit; they got line camps the size of your Ladder layout. We better make sure where Sears is. I can pick up his trail from where he dragged Mac last night."

There was no talk as the two men headed up the road in the tepid afterlight of false dawn. They came to the rocky abutment where the three Wagontree men had ambushed the spring wagon, and Catron had no difficulty tracing the ground where Sears' horse had dragged McIver. Afterward the three crewmen had cut south toward Wagontree land. Much of the near-straight trail crossed an almost barren flat stippled by ironwood and mesquite; Rafe was able to track easily from horseback.

Presently he halted and dismounted to check the ground. Here Sears' mount, with its bent-calked right hind shoe, had plainly split off from the others. "The other two went clear on to Wagontree headquarters," Rafe explained. "Sears headed for the lower Salt Creek, meaning he has a berth at the line camp there. Nearest Wagontree camp to your place."

"Then we go there," Soderstrom said grimly. "I want only Sears."

Rafe stepped into his saddle and settled an uneasy glance on the older man. "You mind saying what you got in mind when we find him?"

"Wait and see, mister." Soderstrom reined on toward the straggling line of the Salt Creek. They followed it for a mile or so and came into the long narrow valley where the Wagon-tree lineshack lay. Tying their horses in a thin skirmish line of timber, they waited for the gray light to give vague form to the shack and its outsheds.

The place lay dark but not deserted; animals were stirring in the corrals. The shack was widely exposed on all sides where brush had been cleared away, and out beyond this the brush flourished in a dense and tangled perimeter. Soderstrom inspected the layout and in several spare phrases told Catron exactly what they would do.

When true daylight paled the east and outlines gained sharp profile, he gave the order. Rafe made off toward the left through the brush, Soderstrom to the right, crouching low. When he was less than fifty yards from the shack, Soderstrom chose a vantage point and sank down on his haunches. He dug out three boxes of shells from his jumper pocket and broke them open. Afterward, rifle across his knees and biting his pipestem, he waited. The air was cool and still. Soderstrom breathed of it deeply; the rifle had an easy, accustomed feel against his palm.

The shack door opened and a man stepped into the yard. He was shirtless, and he looked about and yawned and scratched his gray underwear above his ribs. Afterward he sauntered off toward the corral and leaned on a pole. Soderstrom carefully put his pipe away and sighted up, levered in a shell, and fired.

Splinters flew less than a yard from the man's hand. Even in the still-ghostly light Soderstrom saw his jaw drop, and then he wheeled and lunged for the shack. Deliberately Soderstrom shot again; the man fell grabbing his leg, and a hoarse, panicked cry escaped him.

The door burst open and Richie Sears and another man

53

came out, guns in hand. Now Rafe's rifle spoke from the brush off east of the shack, kicking up dust in front of them. Sears, moving like a lean ghost, sprang back inside. The other hesitated and moved toward the fallen man. Soderstrom fired again and the rider swore loudly and wheeled into the shack, banging the door. The man on the ground continued to groan his fear and pain.

Soderstrom put two shots into the shack door and then rose and loped off, low bent, to a fresh position. Rafe was laying down a steady hammering fire at the east wall now. Crouching in a fresh spot, Soderstrom saw a rifle barrel nudge across the front window sill and bead on his former position. He fired and heard a savage curse as it was withdrawn.

They peppered the windows and the weathered walls with a steady fire, and after a brief rally the two occupants quit shooting. Soderstrom guessed they were both hugging the floor to avoid the slugs that found cracks and windows—his, for Catron was carefully laying his shots high. Now Rafe put a casual fire on the smokestack till it broke and clanged and clattered off the roof. Soderstrom shoved in fresh shells and turned his attention on the door, smashing the upper, then lower, hinges. The bottom one broke and the door fell crazily askew of its own weight. He felt a deep pleasure in this destruction.

"All right—all right!"

There was a note of sheer panic to that yell from inside—it did not come from Sears—and Soderstrom shouted for Rafe to hold fire. He called to the two men to throw out their guns and come out with hands high. After three rifles and a pair of handguns had been tossed out a window, they emerged. Sears held his hands shoulder-high. The other man was clutching a bloody arm and a blood-soaked bandanna was tied around his scalp.

Soderstrom and Rafe both stepped out to view, moving in from either side. Abruptly Richie Sears spun sidelong, running almost double-bent for the brush. Soderstrom yelled for Rafe to hold fire, and Sears crashed into the brush and wallowed through it. "Get your horse and bring him back," Soderstrom called, adding, "I don't rope so good."

Rafe grinned his understanding and wheeled, dashing back toward his ground-hitched animal. Soderstrom approached the two wounded men; he motioned at the one on the ground and said to the other curtly, "Tend him."

The thin rider with the bloody scalp knelt to examine the other's leg. His probing fingers drew a hoarse yell of pain; the man's face was pasty. "Busted," the thin rider said. "All to hell, it feels like." He looked at Soderstrom. "No call for that, mister. We're just working hands, him and me. He needs his leg. If he don't lose it altogether, he maybe won't use it again."

Soderstrom's eyes were flinty. "You should of picked your company better, him and you."

The thin rider cursed him, then dug out a pocket bandanna and started to tourniquet the wound. "Hold on now, Joe. She is got to be tied off."

Rafe was breaking brush in a careless gallop, and now he came into the clearing and streaked past them, swinging his coiled rope. Again the brush swallowed him, and his crackling passage through it followed west across the valley. Unless Sears had managed to reach the hills that bounded the valley, he would be run down in short order.

Then Rafe was circling back, and in a minute he rode into the clearing with Sears dragging at the end of his dallied rope. Sears lay belly-down panting after Rafe halted; he rested on his elbows and spat dirt. He had taken a few bruises, but Rafe had hauled him not very fast over soft ground. It was Soderstrom whom Sears eyed with an unflinching hatred; he spat again.

Without a word Soderstrom went to the brush corral and drove out the horses, hoorawing them off. Afterward he gathered up the guns the men had thrown out, then tramped into the shack and dropped them on the floor. Picking up the heavy lamp from the table he broke it against the wall; he struck a match and tossed it in the streaming coal oil. He wheeled outside then and walked over to Sears, saying, "Get up," in a quietly savage tone.

Sears staggered to his feet and Soderstrom removed Sears' belt and roughly secured his hands at his back. The shack was spewing oily billows of smoke backed by a wicked crackle of flames as Soderstrom, with a word to Rafe, skirted it. Rafe followed him on horseback, tugging Sears along. By the holding corral a lone big cottonwood flourished and sometimes dropped a scanty shade for the corraled animals. Here Soderstrom stopped. "Give me the rope."

Rafe, not understanding, said, "What?"

"The rope," Soderstrom snapped. "Then step down. I will want your help."

Rafe's weathered face altered with comprehension. "You ain't meanin' this."

For answer Soderstrom jerked the noose that circled Sears' chest and arms up around his neck, then secured it with a fixed knot. "I am going all the way, mister. If you don't like it, clear out."

"But God, Mr. Soderstrom! That is plain-out murder. You'll get strung up yourself for it."

The insensate rage held in a tight ball in Soderstrom's belly snapped its thin checkrein and he walked straight toward Rafe. Catron quickly threw down the rope half he still held coiled. He reined off as Soderstrom bent to pick up the rope but did not go far, watching in mounting disbelief as Soderstrom tossed the coils over a spreading limb, then seized the end and drew the rope up tight.

Sears' head was pulled tightly at an angle to his body. All the intensity had washed out of his bright lizard's eyes; they held a total hopelessness that went beyond fear. Sears expected to die now, and he was not afraid. Somehow this cooled Soderstrom's rage back to a simmer, and the sense of Catron's last words reached him. *But by God, I will serve him and his big boss a lesson they will not forget.*

He leaned his weight on the rope and stretched Sears' wattled neck. The man gagged and began to choke. His face darkened; his eyes started to glaze over, and only then was Soderstrom about to ease off. But Rafe Catron shouted with a wild timbre, "Jesus! That's enough, Mr. Soderstrom. Let it up!"

Soderstrom turned his head and saw that Catron's face was dead white, and that he had his six-gun out and loosely pointed. Deliberately Soderstrom turned his back to Catron and gave the rope more pressure. Sears was in the first throes of real strangulation, face purpling and tongue distended, before Soderstrom finally released the rope. Sears' legs folded and he slipped to the ground, retching and gasping.

Soderstrom looked again at Rafe Catron who sat his saddle with the gun limp in his hand, his face etched with sour defeat. "You still working for me, Catron?"

"Sure," Rafe said sullenly. "I guess so."

"Then hear this," Soderstrom said gently. "You ever pull a gun on my back again, you better use it." Turning on his heel, he walked back to the burning shack. The two Wagontree hands were silently watching the shack and all their belongings go up in smoke.

"You men know why this happened?"

"We know," the thin rider said bitterly. "Sears told us. Goddamn his kind, and damn the old man for taking them on."

Soderstrom said, "You might find other ranges more to your taste," and went back to the tree. Sears was sitting with his knees drawn up, wheezing fitfully; his sick eyes turning on Soderstrom held the same fearless hate.

Soderstrom untied his hands. "Get up. Take off your boots first." Sears wordlessly jerked them off and stood up in his sock feet. He flexed his thin hands; he seemed to have an idea what was coming. Soderstrom nodded brusquely to Catron who was looking on dourly. "All right, now we are done here. Get my horse. We go now to Wagontree."

For a moment Catron was speechless. "But what the hell for?"

"I want this old man, Buckmaster, to see his prize gunman who has walked maybe three-four hours with a rope on his neck and no boots."

Richie Sears said in a paper-dry drone, "Don't do that, mister. Not to me."

Soderstrom ignored him. "Most of the Wagontree people will be out on roundup, eh? The few that are left we can handle." He saw Rafe's hesitation and said flatly, "Mister, I asked you if you was still working for me. Now I do not ask, I tell you. Take my orders or get out for good."

"All right." Catron's voice was low and harried. "But you push a man, by God. You push a man."

"There, mister, you are damned right."

Seven

Having forestalled trouble from the two hands by driving off the horses, Soderstrom pushed unhurriedly toward the southwest and Wagontree headquarters. Sears walked ahead of them, the rope on his neck fastened to Soderstrom's pommel. He carried himself as straight as a ramrod in his humiliation, but this was only the start of what he would endure.

They rode downcreek unspeaking, until Rafe ventured carefully, "That was going too far. Busting that Joe's leg and then burning all their stuff."

Soderstrom turned slowly to stare at him. "You joined me to see them get hit. Now I am hitting them, don't read me no scripture."

"I want to see the Buckmasters hurt, sure," Rafe said sullenly. "But these was just poor hands, like I been myself."

"You think Sears is another grubby hand, too, eh?"

"No. Hell, I fancy doing for him myself but not enough to swing for it. I thought of that."

"So did I. But till I did, what I done was my business." Soderstrom's voice was grim. "You pulled a gun on my back."

Rafe traced a callused thumb along the rope scar on his throat. "I had a taste of a rope. That is a godawful way to punish a man. I couldn't think of nothing else."

"Next time you better think only of what I said."

The brisk pace afoot was beginning to tell on Sears. Like

any rider he walked as rarely as possible; his feet were tender and misshapen from years in tight vain cowman's boots. They hit a stretch covered with coarse gravel and sparse bunchgrasses; Sears began to stumble. Whenever he slowed down, Soderstrom gave a vicious flick to the rope, urging him on. Then Soderstrom halted his horse, bringing Sears to a painful stop. A rider had topped a ridge fifty yards away and was coming on at a rapid lope. Rafe shaded his eyes, and after a moment said, "That's Chad Buckmaster."

Soderstrom lifted his Winchester from its scabbard and laid it across his pommel, waiting. The rider pulled up his well-gaited black some yards off; he sat his saddle with an easy grace. He was about thirty and gave the impression of being big all over though his flanks and waist were spare as whipcord. Black curling hair lay like a close cap against his head, from which his ears were faintly batwinged. His face was heavily handsome; he wore a faint provocative smile. His calico shirt, rawhide chaps, and flat-crowned hat were those of any working hand; the thick dust coating them indicated he was on roundup.

The younger brother, Soderstrom thought. Chad Buckmaster was dark like his brother Garth, with much of Garth's considerable size; his smiling and unruffled stare reflected the pleasant irony of his sister Hannah. But he bore little real resemblance to either one; there was a feel about him of potential for either good or bad; you couldn't be sure.

Chad Buckmaster said lazily, "Hello Rafe," and passed a half-shuttered look over Soderstrom. "Ah, the neighbor. Not planning to pay a call like this, were you, neighbor?" Without waiting for an answer, he tilted a nod toward the spume of lifting smoke at their backs. "I was coming to see about that. Our linecamp, I believe." He cocked his head almost politely. "Your work?"

"We will talk on that maybe, when Rafe has taken your pistol."

Young Buckmaster clucked his tongue with a wry grin and shrugged, turning his hands upward. Rafe rode close and disarmed him, ramming Chad's gun in his own belt.

"I'm Chad Buckmaster."

"It is your pa I want to see."

"All right," Chad said agreeably. "I'll take you to him. But not so you can gun him in his own house."

Soderstrom gestured toward Richie Sears. "Is he dead? The other two at the lineshack, they are alive also. But next time it will be different. That is what your pa must know. Maybe if I tell him myself, he will believe it."

Chad frowned slightly, checking his fretting black. "I don't understand this. Something happen?"

"I will talk to your pa only."

"Sure thing," Chad murmured. He fell into loose pace with their mounts as they moved on.

Soderstrom gave him an oblique cold study, saying, "Your big brother is the wolf maybe and you are the rabbit, eh?"

Chad turned his head, smiling handsomely. "The diplomat, let's say. Pa sends Garth when he wants to show his teeth."

"Your brother keeps busy then."

Chad laughed. "Well, he is generally moving some. Look, I want to show you something. Mind turning enough to top that rise yonder?"

"Lead on, but no tricks, mister." Soderstrom guessed from the drift of sound beyond the rise what Buckmaster wanted him to see, but he was still curious.

They swung slightly east and swerved onto the long height that terminated the high rolling land toward this end of the valley. Soderstrom had his first look at a big roundup camp. It lay in a mile-long dip laced with scrub juniper. At one end was the remuda corral filled with fresh mounts, tended by three wranglers. A hundred yards on, the vast sprawl of the camp proper began, a hodgepodge of warbags, spare saddles, blankets, and assorted gear. At one side stood the freight-, chuck-, and calf-wagons with their tailgates down. Two swampers were unloading a wagon, and the cook and his roustabout were butchering a calf. Over the far flat hung an alkaline haze of dust, making half-visible a panoramic bee-hive of activity—flickering branding fires, the black bodies and white faces of countless cattle, the shadowy forms of riders moving back and forth.

Chad Buckmaster said idly, flicking his horse's mane with

his quirt, "That's what you have picked a fight with, my friend. Something to think about, eh?"

Soderstrom could see that the burning of one lineshack made a very minor fleabite on this empire. He gave a stony nod that was also a gesture to motion them back off the slope. Again they set off southwest by the sun.

Richie Sears no longer walked with pride; his head hung to his chest, and occasionally he staggered. Chad said with a thoughtful glance at Soderstrom, "A long way to herd a man like this. We won't be in sight of headquarters in some three hours or more if—"

"Good."

There was no more talk. Sears plugged doggedly on, never looking backward. The sun broiled overhead. Soderstrom called a horse rest finally, and the men dismounted to stretch their legs. Sears collapsed on the ground, his chin on his chest. Chad Buckmaster uncapped his canteen and drank, then said mildly, "Mind if I give him—"

"Not a drop." Soderstrom noticed that the bottoms of Sears' socks were shredded to nothing and the dirt-ground soles of his feet were scratched and bleeding. When he gave the order to go on, Sears climbed at once to his feet and began plodding. Oddly, as if getting a second wind, he walked for a time with an erect and even stride. But Soderstrom could see the aching tautness of his neck muscles and knew each step was an effort; occasional dabs of dark wetness stippled his footprints. And then it came to Soderstrom with a dawning unease that Richie Sears was determined not to break, to somehow turn his humiliation into a victory of sorts.

By the time they came in sight of the Wagontree buildings, the gunman's stamina had broken. He was staggering worse than before. But he lurched on until, blindly missing a stride, he pitched on his face. Groaning, he got his hands braced and crawled to his knees.

Rafe Catron swore, and stepped from his saddle. "That's enough, by God. Shoot me or fire me, but I am giving him a hand."

Soderstrom chewed his mustaches. "All right, load him on in front of you."

Sears raised his head. He said in a parched croak to Soderstrom, "Go to hell, you snorky bastard," and stumbled with a violence to his feet. He went on with his body straight, holding his legs carefully stiff as his bloody swollen feet accepted the alternating agony of his full weight.

They had not reached the outbuildings when he fell again and lay quivering against the ground. Again Rafe got down and this time, against Sears' feeble struggling, lifted him to the saddle. Rafe went ahead on foot leading the horse as they threaded into the working part of the ranch.

Soderstrom could not begin to take in the vast maze of barns and stables and corrals. The area comprising the living quarters was set off on a slight incline. As they approached its huge combination stable and carriage shed, a Mexican stableboy came running out.

"The horses will wait, Luis," Chad said as he swung to the ground. "This *pistolero* has sore feet. Take him to the bunkhouse, then get your grandmother to care for him."

"I'll go along," Rafe Catron said, giving Soderstrom a questioning look. He got a curt nod and started to lead the horse away when Chad said, "I'll take my gun now." Again Soderstrom nodded, and Rafe passed over the pistol.

Richie Sears raised his slumped head. His fancy vaquero's outfit was dirty and torn, and his face was drawn with pain. Only his reptilian eyes were unchanging. "Snorky, I'll remember this a long time."

"I think you will," Soderstrom said, and looked at Chad. "This is far enough. I have come so far, now your pa can come here."

Chad shook his head. "Afraid that's not possible. My father has lost the use of his legs."

After a moment Soderstrom nodded, and the two of them rode on to the main house. Catron had once mentioned how Loftus Buckmaster had started with a 'dobe *jacal* and added a room a year ever since. The construction somehow made a pleasant blend with the sage-dotted hillside it followed upward in a rambling sprawl, the lesser rooms terraced along it above the main house and joined by short flights of open steps. The main part was adobe and two-storied with a broad stone porch supporting gallery columns and an iron-railinged balcony.

They were admitted by a young woman in her late twenties whom Chad introduced as his sister-in-law. Garth's wife was rather slight and delicate with a slim pretty face framed by light brown hair pulled back in a Psyche knot. There was a shy meekness about Naomi Buckmaster, and her words were almost inaudible. She trailed a faint scent of heliotrope; her dress of watered silk rustled as she led the way up a short stairway and down a hallway.

An oak-paneled door opened on a broad well-lighted parlor. Garth Buckmaster, massive and bearded, leaned against a fieldstone fireplace scowling into a whiskey glass dwarfed by his thick paw. His glance found Soderstrom bulking in the doorway; recognition came and a savage curse left him.

Soderstrom said, "Do your feet still hurt?"

Garth made a guttural sound, dropping his arm from the mantel. His great weight tensed, coming forward on the balls of his feet. Then a cavernous voice rumbled from a deep armchair, "Hold still, son, damn it. That walk done you good."

The man who had spoken was a bear-huge man, but he was in the twilight of his life. The years had grizzled his shaggy hair and beard, though the fiery black of his eyes was undimmed. His short truculent neck thrust forward a craggy heavy-jawed head. His great-boned frame was shrunken even in the quilted robe he wore, and the big horny hands resting on his knees had a wasted look. His voice was like distant thunder; it fitted his patriarchal arrogance which, a man had to admit, he wore well.

Chad went to the old man's side, and bending over, spoke quietly and earnestly as if to placate him. Occasionally he nodded at Soderstrom. "All right, all right," old Loftus rumbled at last. Chad sat down then, and Naomi Buckmaster also slipped into a chair and made a pretty pose, looking little and fragile in a room with four hulking men.

Old Loftus pierced Soderstrom with a stare. "Heard plenty about you, Swenska. Can see why, now I clapped eyes on you. So you're the man Angus sold out to."

"Maybe," Soderstrom murmured, "you never thought some-one would not sell to you."

"Nope," old Loftus said affably. "Never did. That's plenty small talk; let's have why you're here."

Soderstrom told him and old Loftus chuckled tiredly. "Now listen, I never ordered Early to crowd your boy and I never ordered Sears to give him a Dutch ride. None of my doing."

"Having men shoot up my place my first night there, that was not your doing, too, eh?"

"Hell, yes. But I judged you would crawl out with a mild prodding. You're a real tiger, son. Something else I never counted on." He picked up a hickory cane beside him and butted it to the floor, leaning his wasted hands on it. "Let's quit all this hemming and hawing. You rough up a tough nut like Richie Sears and haze him barefoot into enemy territory to make a point. All right, I'm impressed. Now let's get to horse-trading. I'll buy you out, land, buildings and cattle for fifteen thousand dollars. Fair?"

"Only if I wanted to sell, mister. I don't."

"Just what do you want, son?"

"I will settle for being left alone. Now you know what happens when I'm not."

Old Loftus seemed to deliberate; he thumped his cane gently on the floor. "How much more land will you be wanting?"

"I got all I need."

"More cattle?"

"Maybe a few over the years, if my range can support them. We have modest ways, us Swedes."

Loftus Buckmaster smiled. "Well, that sounds reasonable. How you feel about me rubbing up agin other folks now and then?"

Soderstrom shrugged. "That is their own lookout."

Old Loftus leaned back, still smiling. "That sure does sound reasonable. Don't puff your crop about this, son. Any-thing you can do to me ain't enough to rouse the hackles on a feist. I am just weighing what your dab of a Ladder is worth to me, and it ain't worth the trouble of a fight."

Garth Buckmaster was pacing heavily back and forth; he halted and scowled. "Pa—"

"Shut your mouth," old Loftus said mildly. "You have got my size and Chad has got my brains, but together you don't add up to the man I was. I give you some say-so now and again because you got to learn; won't be nobody to brace your backs when I'm gone. You listen, boy. I always knew when to pull in my horns and when to crowd. That is why I have lasted as well as growed."

Garth dropped his gaze, a flush mounting to his fleshy face. His big hand threatened to crack the glass it held.

Old Loftus seemed suddenly tired; he shut his eyes and let his head drop back. "You got what you come for, Swenska. See him out, Chadwick."

Coming out with Chad Buckmaster into the midday brightness, he found Rafe Catron waiting on the steps. As the three of them mounted and started back among the sprawl of outbuildings, Chad said genially, "Quite a concession from the old man."

"Was it?"

"You're too suspicious," Chad grinned, and pulled up. "Well, I'll leave you here and head back for roundup. If you're going directly to your headquarters, you'll find the road is best." He touched his hat and loped off toward the north.

Soderstrom and Catron left the headquarters on its left flank and put their horses to the wagon road. Rafe said, "The old greaser woman was making a poultice for Sears' feet when I left him. A wonder for easing a man, them old remedies."

Soderstrom, peering down the sun-touched switchbacks of the road, hardly heard him. And shortly Rafe said, "Who is that coming?"

"His daughter."

"Who?"

"Buckmaster's girl. She runs the newspaper."

"Hell, I know that. But man, you have the eyes." Rafe tipped down his hat and squinted at the coming rider, and shook his head. "Yes sir, you have the eyes."

When they met, Hannah Kingery pulled up her sleepy-looking livery nag. Even on horseback, she looked quite statuesque, wearing a gabardine riding habit and a flat-crowned hat. She gave the reserved hello of acquaintance, and then Soderstrom said bluntly to Rafe, "Ride on. I will catch up."

Catron looked curious, but not very; he touched his hat and rode wordlessly on. Hannah Kingery eyed Soderstrom with a thoughtful smile, not disconcerted. "Were we about to ask each other the same question?"

"Maybe. I thought you did not like your pa."

"I don't have to like him to love a place where I grew up. Often I ride out from town, and if my way takes me near, I always drop in. Besides, Naomi—my brother's wife—has been my closest friend since we were children."

"She is not much like you, missus."

"Don't call me 'missus'," she said a shade crossly. "I can't be over eight or nine years younger than you." The wind had whipped fresh color to her face; she tapped a horsehair quirt against her palm. "Everything you say seems to have the bark on it, Mr. Soderstrom."

"That was not meant badly."

Surprisingly she smiled a little. "I know. And you are right, but when we were children there were no other girls of our age about. Besides, she needs a woman to talk with now and then—or she'd go crazy." She watched him coolly. "I wouldn't have taken you for liking him either, or has the gaff gotten so rough you're selling out?"

"Not this year, missus. He has promised to trouble me no more."

"I told you not to—he what?"

Soderstrom told what had happened to McIver and his own retaliation, and Hannah only shook her head. "But surely you don't believe him."

Soderstrom smiled very faintly. "There is a man I can look at eye to eye. Even crippled up—with arthritis?—there is a man. If I have him right, his pride is too big for what he says. Also if one man could laugh in his face and make it stick, others will know they can. That is why he must drive me off and why today settled nothing. But if I wanted to put a man off his guard, I would tell him otherwise. If I didn't think he would believe, still I would tell him so."

"Of course," she said without inflection. "I said you were alike, didn't I? As a journalist, or snooper, may I inquire as to how Pa has gone about making your life pleasant these last weeks?"

Soderstrom frowned and lifted his shoulders. "He has done nothing. Except to have my place shot up the first night, and then Catron came and drove his men off—"

"I meant to ask you about Catron. He's a suspected cow thief, you know."

"He says he stole nothing. He has worked well and hard, and now I will need him to get my cows to Taskerville."

"You're driving there soon? Be careful. Cattle in a herd are rather a handy target; possibly my father was waiting for something of the sort." She seemed to hesitate. "By the way, your daughter visited me in town yesterday. And you're scowling again."

"*Ja*, so?"

"I was about to ask where she will stay while you're on the drive. Surely not at the ranch."

"She won't. She will come along and drive the wagon with the grub and blankets."

"I suggest that she come to Mimbreno and stay with me while—"

"It ain't I want her doing man's work," Soderstrom said roughly. "I need my three men to herd the cows, and someone must drive the wagon."

She gave him a careful, silent regard. He felt strangely uncomfortable; he had seen no women in weeks outside of Thera and now Naomi Buckmaster, and neither of them had made him aware of his grimy, unshaven, and work-wasted appearance.

"Oh, I see. You're afraid of my influence on her. Isn't that really the thing?"

Soderstrom's first impulse was to growl a denial, but he was uneasily aware of the deep impression this woman had made on his daughter. He liked directness and honesty, and

67

he would not repay Hannah Kingery with less than she had shown.

"What you do," he told her flatly, "is not fit work for a woman."

"My husband was a printer and I assisted him until he died and left me that modicum of experience and nothing else. How would you suggest I make a living, Mr. Soderstrom?"

"Usually a young widowed woman marries again and makes a new home. My mother, my wife, they were good women who worked hard to make their homes good ones."

"Yes," she said coldly. "And died quite young, I shouldn't wonder."

Soderstrom's face closed like a mask; he started to ride on, and swiftly she reached out a hand. "Oh, please—I'm sorry. I did not mean that as it sounded. But a new day is coming for women; young as she is, a girl of Thera's spirit is bound to be caught up in it. Sir, you can't stop it from happening."

Soderstrom snapped, "Happening don't make any damnfool thing good," and put his horse past her on the road.

Eight

In a few days Soderstrom, Catron and Waco Millard had finished up the beef gather. On the evening that they drove the last of the cattle into the holding canyon, a rough count was made. A dozen or so sick and near-starved ones were culled out. They had already separated and branded the late calves and hazed them loose into some coulee cutbacks. These would be turned onto Ladder's open range later, now that the beef cut was complete.

For these last few nights, the three men had made camp close by the holding canyon, splitting up a night watch into three two-hour shifts. So far no sign of trouble; but as he squatted by the fire tonight, brooding at the crumbling cherry coals, Soderstrom's thoughts budged dourly to Hannah's warning that a herd on the move would make a prime target. Rafe came from checking the horses; he hunkered by the fire, lifting the boiling coffeepot in a callused hand impervious to heat, and filled a cup. Against the night chill he wore a bulky coat of goathide with the hair side turned out. He took a deep swig of the scalding brew, burned his tongue, and swore.

Soderstrom took out his pipe, but did not light it. He rubbed it between his palms, staring into the bowl. "Millard is keeping good watch by the canyon?"

"Don't worry. He knows what's at stake." Rafe scowled into the cup, nursing his burned tongue. "We both do."

I wonder if you do, Soderstrom thought grimly. He had a prize crew in this pair, two men moved only by a feral hatred for Wagontree and Buckmaster. Not that this counted against them; he wanted men with the stomach for a fight. Then there was McIver who, he grudgingly had to admit, had turned out far better than he had expected, though he would be in no shape for the drive.

Catron said, "With the calves and culls all separated, about four hundred head for market. We come across enough carcasses and leavings that I'd allow for a heavy kill, but we got more than three men can rightly handle anyway. You want to leave at first light, I reckon?"

"What do you think?"

"My old pappy always said, 'Leave the boss say it, son, and keep your nose clean.' " Catron grinned, then lifted his head. "Sounds like the wagon."

Soderstrom came to his feet, listening as he peered across a star-silvered meadow. Thera, who had stayed at the ranch tending the wounded McIver, was to have arrived earlier today with a wagonload of supplies. Now as she wheeled into the firelight and halted the team, he was surprised to see McIver beside her on the seat. She dropped lightly to the ground, distress in her face. "I did not want him to come," she said, watching McIver carefully step down.

The boy's left arm was in a sling and he moved as if his

body were one vast ache. His stitched and half-healed face was very pale as he limped to the fire. "I am ready to return to work, sir," he said, and Soderstrom only grunted. Rafe gave both of them a mildly incredulous glance, then quietly spat, tossed out his coffee dregs, rose and walked away to his soogans.

When McIver had spread his blankets by the fire and dropped into a fitful sleep, Thera murmured, "I would not say it before and shame David, but Papa, you must send him back to the ranch. He is still sick. He can get about a little, but he must have rest now. When we get back—"

"I tell him nothing," Soderstrom said roughly. "He hired on to work; if he cannot work, let him say so."

"But he will not." Thera's voice held a puzzled, injured note. "You know he won't, a young man so proud. Only if you say to go back, then he will. Won't you tell him?"

"Let him say it," Soderstrom said flatly. He rapped his pipebowl against his boot from habit, then stood up. "No more of this."

She stood too, the pink firelight glinting on her sudden tears. "I thought maybe when you were so mad because they hurt him ... but no, you never cared about David being hurt. I know that now. It was just that they spit in the eye of Soderstrom."

"Thera!"

But she had already swung away and, without looking at him again, walked to the wagon and got her blankets. Soderstrom bit deeply into his pipestem. There was both a curse and a cry in his thoughts, and he could give voice to neither.

Thera, beating a ladle on a skillet, roused them out in the gray dawn. She had a coffeepot bubbling on banked coals and leftover son-of-a-gun stew (as Rafe considerately described it for her ears) warming in the Dutch oven. Within the half-hour they were on the move, driving the small herd out of the box canyon; they swung up through a wide draw and followed it out of the rough country to the flats beyond. Rafe and Waco took the points while Soderstrom and McIver ate dust in the drag. Thera followed fifty yards behind with the wagon.

At Rafe's suggestion, they were avoiding the regular cattle route at the outset. They would make a wide loop north and later swing back toward the trail. Wagontree had probably kept a watch of sorts on their operations and would know they were ready to drive. But Wagontree would have the old trail spotted, and the longer they could be thrown off, the wider Soderstrom's margin of safety. There was no need to scout the terrain ahead; Rafe knew the country well, and had every draw and pothole mentally charted. He allowed that it would make for some mean travel, but there was good grass here and there, and he knew the waterholes.

But as the day wore on, Soderstrom began to uneasily feel that the good prospects had been exaggerated. By his admission, it had been a long time since Rafe had covered this country, and this summer had been unusually hot and dry. Scattered patches of graze gave way to stretches where bone-dry dust rose in impalpable clouds around the plodding beefs, choking animals and riders. The horses had to work without relief, since there was no spare string. The men dismounted from time to time to clean the clogged dust from their mounts' nostrils. The furnace-like heat danced in shimmering waves on every side, and the sun reflected off the alkaline *playas* with a dazzling whiteness that hurt the eye. The men sweated and coughed through a fog of heat and dust, and hoorawed the cattle from parched throats.

Rafe gave the orders, bawling them in husky volleys. He dropped back and told McIver to take over at point. The boy was in bad straits, hunched deeply in his saddle, and he roused himself sluggishly, barely raising his head, at Rafe's voice, then reined over to the position vacated by Rafe.

Soderstrom knew that it was no place for a green rider, and he ranged over by Rafe to say as much. Rafe's grimace cracked the dusty mask of his face. "Jesus, Mr. Soderstrom, you think this eating dust is for a sick man?"

"You want to eat his dust, mister, you do it, but anything goes wrong on his point, it's on your head."

"He'll do all right. Anyhow we're crowding these mossies

too hard. Let's ease down. This is a spooky bunch, and there's a way to push before nightfall."

"You said Lost Sink is the first good water?"

Rafe nodded, wiping a hand over his mouth as he squinted off at the horizon dancing in the heat. "I hope. Seen three-four dried-up seeps already. Water in the Sink will be down, more than like. Never knew her to go dry, though."

The apprehension was more than justified when, toward sunset, they drove the herd up over a sandhill and saw below nothing but a shallow bowl of mud rimmed by white mud that was dried and sun-cracked. Lost Sink had gone dry. Soderstrom put his horse around the flank of the herd, squinting his way through the haze of wind-tattered dust. It made dim forms of the lowing, thirst-crazed cattle, milling back and forth.

When he reached Rafe, the redhead was sitting his horse and softly, monotonously taxing his spare but evil vocabulary. "Bad mistake, and it was mine. Them beefs was thirsting enough this morning they should of been driven to water first, but I thought Lost Sink'd be water high anyways."

Soderstrom's jaw was ridgelike under its dust-powdered beard, but this of all times allowed no luxury of temper. He squinted against the bannering dust from eyes red-rimmed with sunglare and said softly, "The thing is, what now, eh?"

"There's a choice. We keep pushing the way I mapped her and hit Pima Tanks by tomorrow noon. Take the chance the Tanks ain't down, too. If it is, these critters won't last it out. Else we swing around back the way we come and hit the regular route. Hate to think of that, now we come this far, and we're driving enough tallow off these scrubs as it is."

Soderstrom thought it over. "All right, tonight we bed down here. You get a couple hours' sleep and ride on ahead to check Pima Tanks. You will be back before dawn, then we can lay the plans."

Rafe glumly assented, and they herded the cattle on to a good-sized flat below a looming granite ridge. They made camp under the rim and drove the horses back into a narrow fissure in the cliff wall. Here was grass, and a small spring bubbling out of the rocks. They washed their faces and drank their fill, except for McIver who tumbled into his soogans like a drugged man and fell asleep at once. When they had wolfed the simple meal Thera prepared, Rafe also sought his blankets for some sleep preparatory to his long ride.

Thera carried the dishes and utensils back into the canyon and washed them at the spring. Waco Millard was saddling up for nighthawk duty as she returned, her arms loaded, and he said in a shrill half-whisper, "Mind how you set them things down, Missy. Recollect one night on the Red, back in '68. I was with a trail crew pushing a thousand head to Abilene. Quiet night like this one. Fool roustabout was stashing away pots and pans and dropped a whole armload. Cattle was bedded down a half mile off, but the sound set 'em off like Chinee firecrackers. Two men got killed trying to turn 'em."

"Thank you, Mr. Millard." She laid the utensils down carefully, one by one, on the outspread pack tarp. Waco nodded, his scarred face grotesquely twitching, and then mounted and rode out to the skittish, lowing herd.

Soderstrom lay stretched out, head propped on his saddle, puffing at his pipe. Millard's words made him thoughtful; everything depended on this herd, and the number of things that could go wrong made unpleasant thinking. He had kept an eye out all day for any sign that they were being followed. He had seen none, but if Wagontree had been watching them off and on and had caught his herd heading out today, they might have followed up at any distance simply waiting their chance. Hannah had warned him that her father could be holding off only in anticipation of a moment when the herd would be vulnerable. But Soderstrom was satisfied with this bedground; he had open country on three sides and a cliff at his back. There was a full moon. What could the Buckmasters try?

He dozed that way, awkwardly propped against his saddle. When he woke, his neck was sore and stiff; rubbing out the kinks, he became aware of voices. He realized that Thera and McIver were talking on the other side of the wagon, and now Thera was saying in her grave, quiet way, "I wish that you try not to hate my father, David."

73

"I don't—" McIver broke off as if embarrassed, and she, as though he had not spoken at all, went on, "Life has been hard to him. Once he was different, but always he was strong. And when the bad things happened, again and again, because he could not act as a weak man would and let it break him, he could only turn hard. Now that we have come out here, in time maybe the change will turn things different again. I hope for this."

McIver said nothing for a while, as if reluctant to voice a contradiction, and finally he said rather lamely, "I was wondering . . . do you read, Thera? None of my business, except that if you've had no opportunity to learn, I'd be happy to teach you."

"What that says is that my English is so very bad, eh?" He protested, missing the grave teasing in her tone. "No, that's only the truth, David; I was born in America, but Papa and Mama were both from the old country and talked only Swedish at home. So did all the people around where we lived. I did not learn English till I go to school; then it has come hard for I have not needed it till now. I don't think I ever learn English good, David. I read it very bad. I read the Swedish newspapers," she added half-defensively.

"You don't speak English so badly, Thera," he said earnestly. "Why, you know two languages and both quite well; that's an accomplishment. And you can learn to read English as well, if you'll let me teach you."

"Yes," she said very slowly. "I would like this. Then I will ask Hannah to show me how she sets the type. I would like—"

"Who? Oh, Mrs. Kingery." He did not sound pleased. "You want to become a lady journalist."

She laughed. "No. But I have never worked outside my home. This I would like to do, for a little while."

Soderstrom had heard enough; he came to his feet and tramped around behind the wagon. They were sitting tailor-fashion on the ground, and it was all innocent enough, but he felt a slow temper that made blades of his words. "Get out and relieve Millard, college boy."

McIver got gingerly to his feet and limped back into the

canyon to fetch his horse. Thera stood too, saying, "You should not—"

"Be still. You will not hire out to work; I say so and you are my daughter. You hear me good, Thera?"

"Yes." Her face was suddenly very white, but her words held only a proper obedience. "Yes, I hear you."

"And don't ever apologize for me to anyone like I just heard you do," he said harshly. "Never again."

"No, Papa." Her eyes held an icy control, and they seemed to look through him. "I will never speak for you again."

Soderstrom wheeled and stalked back to the fire. The blaze seemed to burn into his eyes; his head started to ache. *Helvete!* Why had he spoken to her in such a way? Maybe Hannah Kingery had been right and he feared losing the one remaining thing for which he cared. Only he had no words to say so, and must fall back on the habit of command. And, in forcing her obedience, was driving her farther and farther from him; but even if the right words had come, he could not have brought himself to say them. Soderstrom sank back on his blankets and, finding no answer, fell into a troubled sleep.

It might have been an hour later that he was sluggishly roused by a hard, insistent hand shaking him by the shoulder. The fire was dead, and dimly now he made out Rafe Catron bending over him. "What—"

"Keep it low, Mr. Soderstrom. Get on your feet, but be still about it."

Soderstrom did, and then whispered, "What is it?"

"Nothing for sure. Was rousting myself to saddle up and heard something make a stir on the rim."

Soderstrom squinted up at the black cliff silhouetted against the stars, a good eighty feet above their camp. He strained his eyes and listened. "An animal."

"On the safe side, would sooner guess it ain't. A fine place for someone to start rolling rock, eh? Better collect the gear and move out quiet as we can. I'll get the horses, you roust out Waco and your girl."

Rafe moved off like a shadow toward the dark mouth of the canyon. Soderstrom yanked on his boots and went to shake

Waco up. The scar-faced man grunted assent to the swift explanation and began reaching for his gear in the dark, rolling it into his soogans. Thera's sleeping place was inside the wagonbed, and Soderstrom had started toward the wagon when he stiffened to the sound of dislodged pebbles rolling down from above.

Suddenly the confined roar of an explosion shook the earth. Soderstrom ran for the wagon with a hoarse yell; he stumbled and fell as a thin shower of stone and earth rained over him. Off right of the camp he heard a massive slab of rimrock shift and tilt and plunge downward. The ground trembled to the impact of collapsing rock. Out in the night, a stir of movement rippled through the herd as the first surge of panic took hold of it. There was a shout and a few shots as McIver made his token effort to contain the panicked animals.

Soderstrom was already on his feet lunging toward the wagon, then was forced to take a sprawling dive to one side, barely in time to avoid being run down by the frightened horses bolting from the canyon, Rafe's savage voice urging them on. At the same time came a roar of grinding rock. Even as he leaped up, Soderstrom was aware that the rotted shale rimrock along this entire section of cliff, weakened by the tremors, was about to go.

Rafe came running from the canyon, yelling, "She's sloughing off on our heads—run for it!" Soderstrom plunged over to the wagon, bawling Thera's name, his words drowned by a thunderous cascade of falling boulders as the rimrock went. A mass of rock and rubble crashed into the wagonbed, and before his mind could even seize on the chaos of what had happened, he was blinded by a rise of bitter choking dust. He felt a tug on his arm. He was obscurely aware, as the roar of the avalanche dwindled off, of a rumble of hooves as the herd juggernauted into a full stampede, but it did not pierce his consciousness.

Rafe was pulling on his arm, dragging him away, and then before the rattle of landsliding rock had died away, the stunning shock of full knowledge brought Soderstrom tearing from Rafe's hold, blindly wheeling back toward the wagon.

The camp was gone, wagon and fire and gear, buried under

tons of massive rubble, the silent dust settling over it. A berserker's roar burst from Soderstrom's chest, a sound of madness and pain that was flung against the cliffs and back.

"Papa—"

He came blindly around, only half-believing his eyes even when he saw her coming quickly, lightly running, from the darkness. He smothered her in his big arms, shaking like a man in fever as he wrested sense from her breathless, broken words. "See, if I hadn't been mad at you . . . so mad I went off walking by myself . . . oh Papa, it is all right!"

Nine

As they squatted around their cook fire in the cool dawn, a kind of sick and exhausted apathy gripped all of them. No one was hungry. They drank black scalding coffee and said little. Beyond the general mood, each of them was preoccupied with his own individual problem; for Soderstrom, it was the recognition of utter defeat.

He couldn't justly attach blame to McIver, since even a number of experienced hands could have done little to halt the wild stampede. By the time he and Rafe and Waco had caught up, the herd had run itself pell-mell into a stretch of razor-edged *malpais* and broken canyons. A number had rushed over sheer drops to death; others, crippled and hamstrung, had to be dispatched one at a time. A few sound head remained, barely enough to bother rounding up. The destruction of the herd, not the herders, had been the Buckmasters' sole intent, otherwise the dynamite charge would have been set directly above the camp.

Hunched by the fire, Soderstrom sipped his coffee and numbly let his scattered thoughts converge. He raised his head, feeling the intent regard of them all and, behind this, a silent question.

"First," he said slowly, "I will go to town and ask the sheriff to do something. He will do nothing. Then I'll have all the excuse I need to hit them in any way I want."

"Well," Rafe said around his cigarette, and paused, squinting against the smoke. "I dunno. We got no proof who dynamited that cliff. Maybe part of what they wanted was to make us redheaded enough to try to settle the score. Be all the excuse they'd need to see us dead."

"You are afraid, then?" Soderstrom's voice was freighted with disdain. "Of them? Of their bought law, eh?"

"Law's still law. As my old pappy would say, don't fancy it and don't buck agin it, either. Anyway we're four men against their whole crew."

"There are ways," Soderstrom said softly. "They like to fight in the dark, eh? Good. Numbers mean nothing in the dark, and it's hard to prove anything. All right, they have shown me the way to fight. And now I have nothing to lose; they have much. That is the way, too." His gaze shot across them. "Well?"

Waco's white hair plumed on the mild wind; his eyes glittered. "That sure shines to me, mister."

Rafe Catron frowned and drew on his cigarette once more, then pinched it out and dropped it. He nodded once; that was all. McIver alone looked uncertain as he raised a drawn and haggard face. "I don't know. I would need time to think about that."

"You have till I get back from town," Soderstrom said, and set down his cup and stood. "Thera will come with me. You men get together what is left of them cows and head them home and turn them loose."

As the two Soderstroms pointed their mounts southeast, Thera made a few attempts at talk, but after a few curt replies, they rode in silence. Obliquely Soderstrom knew that he was letting a feeling of raw defeat crowd him to a reckless action. For last night had seen the ground cut cleanly from under him; he hadn't the funds to make even a start toward restocking his ranch. No matter what sort of fight he carried to the enemy, he could not avoid the overriding, bitter truth: he was finished here. A sense of gray and total futility seized him, but in a minute, remorseless as a sea tide, his unspent rage swept back and held in him like a tight hot ball.

By the early afternoon they reached Mimbreno. The main street, bathing in the heat, was livened by the bustle of Saturday traffic. Rigs and saddle horses crowded the tie rails. Bonneted women flocked the sidewalks in gossiping coveys, and a mob of kids were playing kick-the-can in the middle of the street. They skirted the confusion, and Soderstrom pulled up by the hotel, a two-storied and unpainted building weathered and warped past any redemption of paint or whitewash. His gaze angled across the way to the tie rail of the Alhambra Bar. Among the animals tied there was Garth Buckmaster's big black. He and maybe some other Wagontree men were off to an early start this payday, and Soderstrom thought, *Yes, they would be celebrating,* and felt the anger lift like flame, high and scouring.

He swung to the ground and helped Thera dismount. "Go and get us two rooms," he told her. "Then wait for me."

Her eyes searching his face held a half-plea, and he could read the thought which by now she knew better than to voice; it would do no good. Her eyes were sad and troubled, and she went slowly up the steps into the hotel.

Soderstrom went to the livery and left their horses, and came back downstreet carrying his saddlebags and rifle. Then, seeing the giant form of Garth Buckmaster leaving the Alhambra, he quickened pace. Garth swung around the tie rail to his black, caught up his reins and was swinging heavily astride when Soderstrom came swiftly up behind him. Without a word he reached a long arm and hooked his fingers in Garth's belt and gave a savage yank, stepping back.

Garth plunged backward into the dust. He scrambled onto his hands and knees with a roar. Then grew awkwardly motionless as Soderstrom's rifle was rammed against his ribs.

"You have wiped me out, mister. Maybe I should wipe you out."

Garth's eyes rolled and lifted; sweat and dust stained his shirt and the side of his bearded face. He tried to rumble a laugh, but one look at the hard and angled face of the man above him shut it off.

"This way is too easy," Soderstrom said softly. "Get up." He saw that Garth was not wearing a pistol. He backed off and leaned his rifle against a tie rail post. Garth floundered onto his feet, and then he did laugh.

Krag Soderstrom was big, but this man was like a young mountain. But Soderstrom's mood was jagged enough for him to shrug away any concern at all. He trusted his own reflexes, and he was light on his feet for a man of size.

Buckmaster was still making humorous noises as he shed his coat and, while his arms were locked in the sleeves, Soderstrom stepped easily into him. He drove his right hand into Garth's belly, rocked his jaw with a hard left, and stepped back out of reach.

Garth gave back a couple steps, more surprised than hurt. Blood sprang from his split lip; a slow fury kindled in his eyes. He dropped his coat. He shook his head like a bull and moved in with his great arms windmilling, and Soderstrom sidled away. He feinted low and darted in a hard high right that bounced off Garth's cheekbone. Garth bored in with a feral growl and caught Soderstrom under the ear with a full roundhouse. Earth and sky pinwheeled in pain; he was going down; he hit the dirt. But the impact seemed perversely to clear his head.

Soderstrom rolled up on his knees and onto his feet and the clean hot anger scouring his veins left no room for pain or doubt, only a dogged and wicked determination. Garth moved in swinging, and Soderstrom ducked under his arm and sidestepped him again, then fell into a circling backaway that drew Garth after him, awkwardly circling, too.

Soderstrom hooked a few tentative jabs at his thick sweating face to bring Garth's guard up and, mostly to feel out his defense, whipped a low punch into Garth's belly. He saw Garth's grimace of hurt, and then Garth tried a smothering attack to drive him backward. A glance over his shoulder told him that Garth meant to back him against a building, and he smiled and shifted away, letting Garth carry the attack, but forcing him always into a broad circle.

Garth was in bad condition. He had natural beef and maybe a rough-and-tumble background, but being a gentleman rancher had helped him go slack. His breathing was labored and whistling now, and there was a perceptible drag in his long, sledgehammer swings. Now that it was easier to evade his lumbering enemy, Soderstrom could feel the second strength of his own hard, durable life swaying a slow balance.

He watched Garth's face till a flicker of decision warned him. When Garth charged him suddenly, Soderstrom simply sank his head and let the blow slip off his shoulder and graze his jaw. He moved backward again, but not quickly now, landing a couple of light jabs and one hard hook, drawing Garth into a final furious rally. Garth's belly was not his strongest point, and Soderstrom concentrated on feinting him wide open.

When he saw his chance, he timed the low body smash exactly. It stopped Garth in his tracks and left him slightly bent, hands dropped to cover his belly. Soderstrom took enough time to set his stance and swung, putting his weight behind his arm and shoulder. The blow took Garth on the point of his shelving chin and snapped his head back; his legs buckled and he fell to his knees and pitched on his face in the dust.

Soderstrom stood a moment getting back his breath, then moved to his rifle and picked it up, raking the scattering of onlookers with his glance. Several of them looked pleased as Garth dragged himself up, hugging the tie rail.

"If I ever catch you on my land again," Soderstrom said then in a flint-hard voice, "I'll kill you, mister. Or any of your crowd."

Garth lifted his face, holding himself against the soreness of his belly, and he said sickly, "Jail him, Otis."

Soderstrom moved his gaze sidelong till he saw Sheriff Crashaw standing to his right. The old lawman coughed and came forward, and his eyes, Soderstrom saw without pity, were old and tired. When he had told his story, Crashaw said wearily, "You prove Wagontree did that?"

"No," Soderstrom said in a wicked and measured tone, shifting his grip on the rifle. "Ho, Sheriff, what now? You want to arrest me for assault on this citizen?"

Crashaw did not reply, and Soderstrom smiled. "Good. I guess Loftus Buckmaster and me are two make pretty big tracks, eh? You stick to what you do best. Dozing on your big fat star, mister."

He let the dregs of his anger out in cold contempt, then swung deliberately about and walked away. Crashaw said in a tired voice, "Hold on, you." Soderstrom did not even look back. Somebody laughed.

Soderstrom tramped into the hotel lobby, signed for the room Thera had reserved for him, and went upstairs. He paused in the murky corridor by her door which adjoined his, and knocked. She opened the door quickly, and he saw only the good warmth of relief in her expression, and was suddenly grateful that she had the gift of understanding much that went unspoken, he being no man of words. He said gruffly that later they would go down to supper together.

Inside the sweltering cubbyhole of his room he stripped down to the waist, then soaped and washed. The fight had spent his anger to deadness, and he felt a vast weariness as he dried himself on a strip of frayed toweling.

Beating Garth Buckmaster and facing down a sick old man had given him an arid satisfaction but had done nothing to solve his real problem. No matter what vengeful gestures he made now, he was through. Good God, he was supposed to be a practical Swede. More, he was a thirty-seven-year-old widower with a daughter to think of, not some wild buck who could follow up any whim that suited his fancy. Well, what now? He had come to town only to clear his conscience by telling the law what had happened, but maybe while he was about it, he should look for a buyer for the ranch.

This feeling of exhausted defeat had the power to frighten and arouse him; he rasped an angry hand over his whiskers, then got out his shaving kit and soaped his face, setting to with the razor before the lather could soften his beard, liking the keenness of raw steel along his jaw.

Someone tapped on the door and he growled, "Who is it?"

"Hannah Kingery."

Soderstrom told her to wait a minute and got into a clean shirt before opening the door. She stepped inside, and the slatted sunlight promptly brought out her freckles. She was wearing a starched blue dress and a pert straw hat and she looked very slim and supple; she brought a scrubbed freshness and radiance into the drab room, and somehow this disconcerted him. He swung back to the washbasin, muttering gruffly that he had to finish shaving.

"I don't mind." Hannah took the single straight-backed chair and met his eye in the mirror. "I overheard some talk of what happened and what you told Otis, so I quizzed my sterling brother a bit just before he left town. He had a good deal to say, mostly about your ancestry, and was occasionally lucid. Of course he denied dynamiting your herd."

"So, you have come for a story?"

"That can wait," she said calmly. "Now I am interested in hearing whether you can make a comeback. Well, frankly—how do you stand financially? That is none of my affair, but—"

"I am stone broke. I am busted flat." His savage stroke with the razor made a deep nick, and he swore feelingly. All his anger came flooding back. "Your old man thinks he knows what a dirty fight is. He ain't seen a fight, not till I have shown him one. And by God, I will!"

Hannah said calmly, "All right, don't listen."

"What?"

"I was about to tell you of a better way, but don't listen to me. By all means, fight him as you're planning to, and end up in jail or dead."

Soderstrom whittled grimly at his beard for a half-minute, then slowly lowered his razor, thinking, *Damn all your pride; ask her*. "What way is this?"

"The right way. As you were, standing up to him as an honest man on your own land, giving him back all he could give and better."

"Damn it, woman, understand one thing—"

"I know—money. I can loan you all that you need to restock your ranch on any terms that would be convenient."

Soderstrom stared at her quite impassively for some seconds. He concealed his astonishment, but not quite his instinctive suspicion. "Where does a woman who says she needs to work for a living get this kind of money?"

It was Hannah's turn to be disconcerted, and she flushed slightly. "In a way, it was true enough. My mother left me her jewelry . . . I was still in my teens when she died. It was all I had as a remembrance of her, and I tried to retain the collection intact. I had to sell a couple of stones to keep my husband and me alive, and after his death, I gave up several more pieces to buy the *County Press*."

Soderstrom was already shaking his head. "No, keep your jewels. It would not be right—"

"Wait. Listen, please. Any bank in the territory outside of Mimbreno will give you a loan if I cosign and put up such collateral. The collection has been appraised at a value of fifty thousand dollars. We can take the stage to Salt City over east of here and arrange the loan with the bank there."

Soderstrom hesitated, watching her grave freckled face that was not pretty and not plain, and more than merely beautiful. The flat refusal on his lips came out as a temporizing growl. "That is splitting a mighty fine hair for any difference, missus."

"I know," she said quietly. "Look at it this way. Perhaps I am as desperate as you. This is something I must do."

"Against your father and brothers?" An insight came to him, and he said, "You hate your pa that much, eh?"

"I hate his ruthlessness and greed. Is that strange? So do a lot of people." She bit her lip and lowered her eyes, and murmured, "Very clever, Mr. Soderstrom, but it's none of your affair. Does it matter what my reasons are? My offer can save your ranch . . . and there is your daughter's welfare to consider."

He nodded brusquely. "I have considered. I will take the offer of a loan; I will give ten per cent interest and not thank you, since I'm doing you a favor, too, eh?"

"Very well," she said crisply, and stood up. "I would like to make a suggestion . . . and it is only that, a suggestion. You can never hope to rival my father in terms of land or size of herds; but for all his shrewdness, he's old and set in his ways, and the future will belong to those who act now." She hesitated. "You know of the shorthorn cattle that stockmen in New Mexico have been breeding successfully? They're a beef stock far superior to anything ever introduced in this country—"

"Look, I'm not so much of a fool. They are not built for this high country, and they won't weather here."

"That's what all the old-timers say, of course, but as a matter of fact the New Mexico cowmen have raised shorthorns successfully in country and climate much like this. That certainly warrants a try, and I hadn't thought of you as an old man—quite."

Women, Soderstrom thought dourly, had a knack for throwing up a proposal as a challenge seasoned with qualified insult. He held a skeptical silence, and she added sharply, "I was raised on a ranch, and I am not a fool, either. However, if you can't trust a mere woman's word, then ask Rafe Catron. You trust his judgment, don't you?"

"Yes," Soderstrom said stonily. He toweled the traces of lather from his stinging jaw, scowling at the mirror. "I would be on the trail a long time, bringing back this new herd. I would like to leave Thera with you, and I will pay for her keep."

"Why?" she demanded tartly. "I thought you disapproved of my possible influence on her."

"I do not deny it. But a trail drive is no place for a girl. Last night she could of got killed. I thought—" He checked himself. "Will you do this? Not for me—for her."

Hannah said that she would if Thera were willing. Soderstrom called his daughter in to secure her agreement; to his surprise, Thera was hesitant at first. But once convinced of her father's approval, there was a quiet glow in the way she agreed. However, she insisted on earning her keep at whatever work Hannah could assign her. *Newspaper work,* Soderstrom thought, and was not pleased.

After he and Hannah had agreed to take tomorrow's eastbound stage for Salt City to arrange his loan, Soderstrom got some much-needed sleep, and in the early evening, he and

Thera left the hotel for the café downstreet. The rough buildings were mellowed by the late sunlight; thick shadows barred the tawny dust of the street as they crossed. A man hailed Soderstrom and he turned, seeing with impatience that it was the sheriff.

But there was no nonsense about Crashaw as he halted before them. "I been thinking a good while, Soderstrom. There was a time when a man couldn't have spoke to me as you did and lived."

Soderstrom gibed, "That was a long time ago, eh?"

"It was. Maybe that's why what you said was true enough that I can swallow it now. But that ain't what I mean to tell you." The slow iron in Crashaw's voice took on an edge. "What I'm saying now, you make just one move against Wagontree on their patented land and you got a U.S. marshal to reckon with. I'll send for him."

Soderstrom said with a puzzled, mounting irritation, "Maybe you will have a time explaining to him how it is that Wagontree enjoys special favors in that regard, eh?"

"I don't reckon, after tonight. First thing tomorrow I'll head out to see Loftus Buckmaster. I'll tell him what I told you—there'll be no range war in this country while I wear the badge."

"Ho," Soderstrom said with a dry skepticism. "When did you decide to bite the hand that feeds you, Sheriff?"

Crashaw looked off into the growing twilight, and the saffron light was not kind to his seamed face. "I earned that, and expect I'll get more of it. And take it, too." His voice was distant and musing. "A while back I found my thinking getting slow and my hands shaky. A bad thing for a lawman any time, but worse when it makes him run scared. A man getting old is a man can forget when his reputation wasn't up for grabs to any bidder. When the badge meant something because the man behind it did. I ought to thank you, son."

Soderstrom was listening carefully now. The words came from a sick, aging husk of a man, but in them, for the first time, he felt the iron of what the man had been. And he said surlily, "Me, I never asked for the fight."

"You stuck your jaw out far as you could was all," Crashaw

said grimly. "But I'm minding that the trouble was deep before you come here. About your herd—there's no proof who dynamited it. Old Buckmaster will be on my back to serve a warrant on you for assaulting Garth. All I'm serving is a warning. From here on you better consider any score with the Buckmasters to be even. Because I mean to keep it that way. If a federal marshal ain't enough, I'll wire Fort Bowie to send troops and declare martial law. You mark me—this fight's done."

Ten

Thera selected a piece of ten-point type from the typecase dexterously enough, but, trying to slap the oily metal too quickly into the brass typestick, she dropped it. Bending to pick it up, she lifted a flushed face to see if Hannah were watching. Seeing that she was, Thera laughed, and so did the older girl.

"Didn't I say that you handle the type very well?" Hannah chided. "Don't worry about your speed; that will come with time and patience. Dan—my husband—used to say that all typesetters should be women, because they have small nimble fingers."

Soberly Thera spread her fingers out, studying them. "I want to be good. As good as you. There seems so little in the world that a woman can do better than a man." She sighed, and then smiled in an antic way. "I guess there's one thing no man can do, though."

Hannah laughed. "And what would you like to do most?"

"That, I guess." Her smile turned grave. "Be a good wife and mother like my mother was. I think there is nothing better, Hannah."

Hannah went thoughtfully back to her desk and tried

again to develop the germ of an editorial idea, but the approach still eluded her. The lesson she had absorbed from her quiet, quick-witted young helper in these few days still had a raw, rough-edged quality that needed to be shaped and smoothed by familiarity. Not that Thera had expressed any thoughts on the matter; she had simply shown, by her bright and active outlook, her eagerness to learn, that a woman could make a goal of home and husband and babies (as she had guessed of this girl long before Thera had said so) and still make of her life something more than mere drudgery.

This, Hannah had begun to suspect, was her real woman of the future, not the militant feminist who wanted to turn all of her sex into imitation males, thereby defeating her own avowed purpose: the emancipation of woman as woman, of that part of her which man had denied her expression of through the ages.

No doubt, Hannah thought, growing up in the house of an overbearing and lusty male like her father was responsible for her rebellion against male dominance. *By plunging into a bad marriage*, she reminded herself wryly. *So how much do you really know, my girl? About life or men or yourself?*

Impelled by boredom and restlessness, she threw down her pencil and walked back to the print shop to say that she was going out for a while, and could Thera hold things down? The girl nodded, an eager sparkle in her eyes. Obscurely, they reminded Hannah of Soderstrom's eyes, which prickled with the play of heat lightning on the horizon. And not a far horizon, with his temper.

She told herself resentfully that she did not want such a man invading her private feelings. But he was hard to ignore; like her father, he filled the sky wherever he stood, and it was unwise to measure such men impulsively.

Most of the county gossip, since Soderstrom and his three men had departed, had to do with the mild revolution of the shorthorn breed that Soderstrom meant to introduce, and what Loftus Buckmaster would do about it. Popular sentiment more-or-less swung behind the Swede as underdog, but favored her father as the long-run winner, even if this shorthorn thing were not a fool idea. The idea was sound, Hannah thought (with a wry smile since it was her own), but as a pioneer achievement in this part of the territory, it would be both miscredited and blown out of proportion. Krag Soderstrom was the kind of man around whom legend would naturally grow.

The town sprawled like a dozing, slat-ribbed cur in the morning sun as she rode east on a rented nag. The wind was brisk and silky on her face and carried the flavors of the country, and she rode against it with pleasure and forgot time. She came, as she often did, in a circuit of the hilly wilderness around Mimbreno, to the forking at the Wagontree boundary where a lone road switchbacked deep into Buckmaster land to the headquarters. It had been a long while since her last visit with Naomi, she remembered with a trace of guilt, and put her mount down the road.

Just east of the headquarters the road curved sedately around a high eminence of land. On whim, Hannah swung off from the road and climbed her horse to the summit of the giant rise. Here she halted, breathing in the matchless view this promontory had always afforded her. The shallow snake of water that was the lower Salt Creek made its crooked way around and below the hill on this side, and presently she took notice of two horses ground-hitched by a motte of cottonwoods that fringed the creekbank.

I know those horses, she thought idly, without particularly relating either animal to any person. Not until the two owners moved now out of the mottled shade of the trees—a man and a woman. Quite plainly, from the way they were standing together, she had surprised a moment of intimacy.

Hannah dropped quickly back across the brow of the hill, still unseen, and headed for the road. Even when the pair had stepped into view, she would have been hard put, at this distance, to identify them if not for the two distinctively marked horses. They belonged to Naomi and her brother Chad.

What she had seen did not greatly surprise Hannah, yet she was disturbed as she rode slowly on toward Wagontree headquarters.

She felt the familiar, quickening warmth at her first sight

of the old terraced house, and wondered a little, as she always did, that so many of the memories it brought back were good ones. She replied to the Mexican stableboy's pleased greeting, handed him her reins, and walked up to the house.

Loftus Buckmaster was sunning himself in a deep chair on the Spanish veranda, which was rare for him in these days of near-total confinement indoors. The chair gave a protesting creak as he leaned forward watching her sharply, resting his horny hands on his cane. "Good morning, sister."

Hannah nodded briefly, and said, in order not to betray what she had seen by the creek, "I want to see Naomi."

"She's out ridin'. You can wait for her inside, where it's cool. Come along and talk to your old man a spell." Laboriously he heaved to his feet; his great frame showed all the ravages of age and arthritis as he led the way unsteadily into the house, leaning heavily on his cane. He paused to rest halfway on the staired hallway to the parlor, letting his cane take his massive weight; his breathing was harsh and his legs unsteady, and Hannah reached for his arm. "Get your hands off me," the old man snarled, and stamped on to the parlor with massive slow strides, slumping into an armchair.

Hannah took the sofa, glancing about the parlor with its shabby heavy furnishings that had never, within her memory, been changed or even budged from their original arrangement. Unbidden, she had a sharp memory of a Christmas day when she was nine . . . of her father sending out wagons to make the rounds of every poor family in the county, transporting all the children to Wagontree for a party, a turkey dinner and presents and pony rides. *How long ago that was,* Hannah thought, and turned her gaze on this giant, fierce-eyed old man who had fathered her, wondering a little sadly now, *Did you ever really know him?*

"Well," Loftus smiled grimly. "You look to see your friend Soderstrom back soon?"

"I see that your spies have been busy."

"The old man has a few friends here and there in the territory, sister."

"I wonder who," Hannah murmured. "The stage driver? A

90

clerk in the Salt City bank? But what's the difference—you know what to expect, then."

"Shorthorns," Loftus snorted. "Fat, stump-legged brutes. You think they can weather this territory long? No, I got a better question." He picked up a newspaper beside his chair and shook it in a veined hand. "And these damned editorials. What you reckon to accomplish by making a palsied goddamn spectacle of yourself, siding with the old man's enemies? A man's own daughter tearing him down in public is a miserable thing."

Hannah smiled. "Is that what bothers you? And I've been thinking it was my brilliant exposition."

Loftus sighed. " 'Land-devouring monster' . . . 'the modern-day Attila beneath whose galloping hooves of conquest the very grass dies' . . . 'Nineteenth-century Borgias.' That is damned bad writing, sister. You always was a sassy baggage, but it was almost a pleasure to hear, the way you twisted your tongue around words. Only take my advice for once, and break the pen."

Hannah found herself flushing defensively. "Well, that's journalism. And I'll tell you why, since you ask. I hope to get every man, woman and child in the county so inflamed, they'll flood the lawmakers with letters of—"

Loftus broke in softly, impatiently, "Not what I meant. No, I want to hear why you always have to fight the old man. Why you always had to do black when I said white. I'm just a crude old man, sister, but tell me."

"Whose fault was any of it? You pushed me, Pa, as you did all of us."

"Ah, is that the word? But your brothers took it. Seems you never could. Why run off with that printer fellow like you done? A sorry thing, if I reckoned right and you married that gutless boy just to spite me."

Hannah said coldly, "Well, you can always reckon."

"Sister, the old man is tired and he don't want to fight you no more. Quit acting like a bullheaded fool. Sell the damn paper and come back here to live. Things will be different."

Hannah turned her hand over and studied the faint, ineradicable ink stains on her fingers. "Different how, Pa? Can you admit you were wrong?"

Without raising her eyes she felt his slow stiffening, and he said, "I was never wrong. Sorry, yes, if the real mischief was that you took me amiss. But that was your wrong, not mine."

Hannah thought, *He will never change,* but she had already known this much, and she had no more to say. A spell of silence held for some minutes, broken to her relief by Naomi's arrival. She entered the parlor with a quick, eager step, obviously pleased to see Hannah.

"The stableboy told me you were here. Let's go to my room, Han. Will you excuse us, sir?"

At that moment Garth came in, the scowl on his bearded face deeper than usual. "I want to talk to you, Pa." He did not bother to greet Hannah, and she noticed a faint bluish welt on his cheekbone, a fading token of his thrashing at Soderstrom's hands. Garth turned the scowl on his wife. "Your rides is getting too damned long for my taste. You stay nearer the house hereafter."

Does he suspect? Hannah wondered, knowing that Garth's suspicion of an affair between Chad and Naomi, once confirmed, would result in no mild castigation. Naomi's head drooped, and the flushed brightness of her face drained away. Since her marriage to Garth, the life had gradually gone out of this once vivacious and bubbling girl. Thinking of that, Hannah found easy forgiveness for what she had seen by the creek. Remembering her mother, too, she thought then, *No woman can live under this roof and keep her soul intact.*

The two of them went to Naomi's room, which was terraced a half-level above the parlor. Here, once the door was closed and they were safely alone, the tension seemed to leave Naomi. With a vast sigh, she threw her hat at a chair and sank across the bed. Hannah, never one to mince words, thought, *Probably this is none of my business,* and then with a wry self-resignation, *When did that stop you? Get it over.*

"Naomi. What about you and Chad?"

Naomi sat bolt upright. Her whisper was tremulous and dreading. "You knew—Han?"

"It was hard to miss," Hannah said bitterly, and briefly

told how she had come on them by chance. "Dear, I'm not accusing you, or even lecturing you, but you're being very foolish."

"But we love each other, Han." Seeing Hannah's silent but unconcealed skepticism, she said with a kind of defensive desperation, "Chad *does* love me. You don't understand him."

"Just as I didn't understand Garth? I warned you what he was like, too, but you were finding gorillas attractive that season and wouldn't listen. You'd better listen now." Hannah moved across the room and, taking Naomi by the shoulders, shook her gently. "I know my brothers only too well. Don't deceive yourself about Chad. You're desperate and bored, and he's exactly the kind to use that fact."

"No," Naomi said sullenly. "You're wrong about Chad. That's all you see because you won't look any deeper."

Hannah sighed her exasperation. "Put him to the test, then."

"What do you mean?"

"Tell him to take you away from here, away from Garth and Wagontree. You should have left Garth long ago, anyway."

"Oh no!" A bright terror blazed in Naomi's face. "I'd be afraid. Garth would hunt us down if it took him forever."

"I would hazard," Hannah said dryly, "that you and Chadwick have discussed the matter, and that is what Chad said?"

Naomi flushed and said resentfully, "You're unfair to us both, Han."

"Not to Chad, not ever." Hannah pressed her shoulder gently. "All right, I'll say no more about it. But be more careful . . . if I could come on you so easily, so can Garth or somebody else."

Deliberately, Hannah turned the talk into other, lighter channels; but she had a disturbing conviction that the situation was drifting toward deep trouble. Chad would have private reasons for continuing the affair, and Naomi would be too weak-willed to cut it off.

It was a good two hours before Hannah took her leave. Each separate room in the terraced sprawl of the house had its own outside door, and, in order to avoid a second encounter with her father, Hannah left for the outside by Naomi's

93

exit rather than through the parlor. She followed a flagstone path down the hillside, past the 'dobe main structure that enclosed the parlor and the dining room.

She paused by the wall to curiously watch a horseman who came loping into the yard, his mount's hide fouled with dust and lather. The young rider, as he dismounted by the stable, showed the signs of hard-driven exhaustion.

Leaving his horse with the boy, he headed immediately for the house, removing his dusty hat to beat it against his chaps. He had obviously come a long way in a hurry, and Hannah's first idle thought, that he had been dispatched home from a trail drive with some urgent message, was discarded. No Wagontree herd took the trail to Taskerville without at least one Buckmaster along; her father and brothers were on the ranch.

Standing as she was, partly hidden by a salt cedar that flanked the wall, Hannah escaped the rider's notice as he tramped onto the porch; she heard the door close behind him. With her curiosity fully aroused, Hannah looked furtively around before sidling over to the east wall window. It opened off the dining hall, and this room and the parlor beyond were connected by an open hallway. The voices from the parlor carried faintly to her ears.

"You sure of this, Sam?" her father was saying.

"Yes, sir," came the rider's drawling twang. "He is rolling up about ten miles a day, while keeping close to good water. Should bring him to the Baxley Peak country by tomorrow night, just about five miles north of the county line. That's what you wanted to know, ain't it?"

"That's it, Sam." Her father's voice boomed with a quiet exultance. "A fair job, watching his moves all this while. Sure you wasn't seen any time?"

"Nary once. I growed up with Injun kids, and I don't make no mistakes."

"What is this, Pa?" came Garth's gruff deep tones. "You got somewhat on the fire you ain't told of?"

"Somewhat, son." Loftus chuckled mildly. "I'm about set to nail Mr. Soderstrom's hide fast to an outhouse door. Don't ever sell the old man short, boy. This goddamn arthritis may hold me down, but it don't put me out."

Hannah could picture Garth's baffled scowl as he growled, "Pa, Otis Crashaw is turned against us. First time you move against the Swede, he—"

"Not outside his own jurisdiction, he don't. Shut your mouth and hear the old man out. I have had Sam here watching the north trail over in Addison County for Soderstrom's herd. He was to follow the Swenska's outfit a couple days and size things, and then report back. You heard him. Soderstrom will make camp hard by Baxley's Peak tomorrow night. You'll be there with six or so men. You'll have to make your play on what you see, but that is rough and wild enough country that I wouldn't be surprised you could run this herd to death like his other one. . . ."

Hannah waited no longer. A sudden fear of discovery knotted in her throat, and she moved on at a fast walk. She forced a casual pace as she neared the stable. The boy, smiling his vast pleasure, went to saddle her mount, and as Hannah waited, she reviewed what she had heard to be sure she had the sense of it. There could be no doubt; Loftus was defying the sheriff's warning by striking a blow at Soderstrom outside the range of Crashaw's authority. Her father could afford to take an extralegal risk or two up in Addison County, where he had friends.

Baxley's Peak by tomorrow night, Hannah mused. And they were covering about ten miles a day, meaning the herd should be bedded at Blue Springs tonight. She stepped up to the sidesaddle and arranged her skirt, barely replying to the boy's happy, *"Buenas tardes."*

A good twenty miles of bad country lay between here and Blue Springs, but she knew most of it like her own hand. Well, why not? Her mount was fresh, and by starting now, she could reach the Springs before nightfall to give Soderstrom the warning he needed.

Eleven

It had been a long day on the trail, for Soderstrom wanted to make camp at Blue Springs. A sooty veil of dusk had fallen, softening the harshness of the land, before they achieved the moon-glimmering spring set in its deep natural saucer. Patiently, they let the herd water, then made camp and wolfed their supper, beans and biscuits. Afterward they sat on their heels by the fire and drank strong coffee and talked. The talk was idle, the sort of needless palaver men made when anything could break and they were keyed for it.

All four of them were honed to a quiet tension, but little of it stemmed from the long day on the trail. Soderstrom had held their progress to easy stages, wanting to wear as little tallow as possible off the heavy-bodied shorthorns. They had been bred for beef, not travel, he thought with satisfaction. Also, mindful of how skittishness from thirst had contributed to the fate of his other herd, he had timed each halt, where possible, close to good water.

It was really a knowlege of their adversary that had laid a shadow of tension over this drive. Tonight they were camped only eighteen miles or so from their home range, with four hundred head of prime whitefaces. And, because he read the man's mind as he would his own. Soderstrom was sure that Loftus Buckmaster would make his move before long. But would he, in the face of Crashaw's warning? *Yes,* Soderstrom thought decisively, *because that would not stop me, either.* Buckmaster could not afford not to act, for he had made his life a boast backed up, always, by his actions; because he was top dog, any man who successfully defied him would topple him: the only law by which such men could live. *We are dying out, me and Buckmaster,* Soderstrom thought with a fleck of grim humor, *but I think we will go down kicking damn hard.*

The move would come soon because once scattered on its home range the herd would be no target at all. Soderstrom hesitated to anticipate beyond this. *He is a sly old devil, so do not be too sure of anything.*

Out in the night Waco, on guard, crooned strangely to the herd. Rafe and McIver carried on an idle, joshing talk to which Soderstrom half-listened with a sleepy ear. In these last days he had been surprised to feel a growing sense of cohesion with these men; but he remembered from his younger days that it was always so with men who had lived and worked together for a good while. The rough edges of each man's character were filed down day by day until the early frictions disappeared and the men were in gear. They were an oddly assorted group, and finding a common level had taken time; by now the tolerations were fairly established.

This fact had enabled Soderstrom to see Dave McIver in a slow-changing light. Against his first dislike, he could not ignore the way the youth had taken what this land had to offer and paid its price in sweat and pain. At times only sheer will had kept him going, but he had won the biggest stake of his life. He had not coughed up blood in weeks; his appetite was hearty, and he no longer thought of liquor. What little excess flesh his ravaged body had carried was gone, replaced by hard spare muscle. The boyish lines of his face had tightened to the sun-blackened gauntness of an Indian's, and it still carried the faint scars of his beating. His young beard, bleached now to almost alkaline paleness, was in startling contrast, and did not quite conceal a new hint of iron around the chin and mouth. Soderstrom noted this, seeing in it the measure of a man finding himself. And, though McIver had education (which was perhaps not so bad a thing) he had never flaunted it. He spoke easily but seldom; he did not smile often either, but when he did, his thin serious face was fairly lighted by a boyish and self-chiding humor. He still wore the derby, discolored and sadly dilapidated now. It was no hat for holding off the sun; it had made him a butt for jeers and gibes since he had come West, yet he had refused to relinquish it. At first it had been a badge of defiance, finally of victory; and nothing could have impressed Soderstrom more.

Rafe got up and said good night, and walked away to his blankets. McIver rose too, then, and when Soderstrom said, "Dave," the college boy's glance held a pure astonishment. Soderstrom hadn't once called him by name.

"You have done pretty well this drive."

McIver eyed him a dubious moment, and finally said guardedly, "Thanks," before moving off. Soderstrom got out his pipe and packed it carefully. McIver was a lot better all right, but, he thought grimly, he would have to be very good to make the grade with Thera. Soderstrom was coming to a reluctant concession that someday Thera, having a mind of her own, would choose a man; and whatever or whoever he was, Krag Soderstrom would have to bow to the inevitable. So far McIver had come off well with her because his weakness had taken her sympathy. Now that he . . .

"Hello," said a woman's hushed voice out of the dark; and Soderstrom was on his feet, whipping up and levering his rifle in the same motion. "Who is that?"

"Well, there's no bounty. It's me, Hannah. Mind if I walk in?"

Soderstrom said gruffly, "Come in," concealing how astounded he was without much trouble because he was deeply nettled at being surprised this way.

After a moment, leading her horse, she entered the rim of firelight. She was wearing a very dirty and sweat-soiled riding habit; the skirt had several brush-tears, and her face was streaked with grime and sweat. The horse was limping, and Hannah promptly sat down, obviously footsore. "I misjudged my bearings and lost the trail, and when I found it again, he threw a shoe. That was just before it turned dark . . . walked ever since. I can smell the coffee. What's in that Dutch oven?"

By this time Catron and McIver were out of their blankets, and they listened intently as she told of her father's plan to waylay the shorthorn herd tomorrow night. Soderstrom asked all the questions he could think of, while she finished the beans and biscuits and had two cups of Rafe's caustic coffee. This was what he had needed to know about the trap he'd been positive would be sprung. All he needed now was a counterplan to meet it.

They talked it over a while, and Rafe and McIver returned to their soogans. Soderstrom said he would go on guard duty soon, and offered Hannah his blankets. "Rafe will fix your horse's shoe in the morning. We packed a few smith tools along with the grub and blankets on a couple horses, since we have no wagon now. How is Thera?"

"I was wondering when you'd ask." Hannah tempered her words with a smile. "She is fine."

"Let's walk a little," Soderstrom heard himself say, and then with embarrassment, "I am sorry. Your feet."

"Are not that sore. You might help me up, though."

They walked slowly down by the spring. The mirror-still blackness threw back the universe: countless white points of starfire. A meteor blazed a pale falling path, and died.

"How do you feel—" Soderstrom paused, scowling at his unlighted pipe. "Don't take this wrong, but I have wondered about your feeling for your pa."

"Oh—you think I'm betraying him now?"

"Not that. Just that the blood tie should mean something."

"It does." She bit the words off with a kind of snap. "Among other things, it meant seeing my mother die year by year because she was one who needed to be loved as a plant needs water. It wasn't even his indifference, bad as that was. He had chosen her as he would a mare he wanted bred. He was already forty, and hard clear through. She was only twenty, and for twenty years after that, she did nothing but die." Hannah was vehement. "Nobody who didn't have to live with it could understand. With his children, it was different, in the sense that he knew exactly what he wanted them to be. You've seen the results. Garth and Chad. Me."

Soderstrom struck a match and coaxed his pipe alight, remarking that he supposed Loftus had been less than pleased with his results.

"I didn't say he was pleased, did I? To escape from him, I did not marry the first man who came along. Just the most

99

spineless one, the most footloose and vacillating, an itinerant printer named Dan Kingery. He was at the other extreme from Pa, but I made Pa's own grand mistake. I would remold this sorry clay into exactly what I wanted.

"It didn't work out quite that way. Drinking is a second occupation with printers—that and traveling. A good compositor can get a job anywhere. And a bottle. That was one thing I couldn't control, and when he became stupefied, he couldn't work. We would have starved more than once if I hadn't sold several of Mother's jewels. At last, in one of his rational periods, I insisted that he show me how to set type. Afterward I was able to finish the jobs he couldn't."

Soderstrom took the pipe from his mouth. "What happened to him?"

"Fell over a stair railing one night, I needn't mention why, and broke his neck. So I came back to Buckmaster County—"

"Why?"

The blunt question made her frown in the starlight. "Why? Because this country is my home and I love it. Oh Lord, never mind. I know what you've wanted to hear me say. All right, I came back here and bought the newspaper less because I needed to make a living than because it offered the one way I could really fight him."

"Hurt him."

"Damn you," she whispered, dropping her face. "Yes, hurt him."

"And did you?"

"He admitted as much to me today," she said wearily. "There was no satisfaction in hearing him say so."

"Then it was all a waste." Soderstrom spoke gravely, and slowly puffed his pipe. "You have called me hard. But you, you set out to hurt your own pa, and it didn't even satisfy you."

"What about you, Mr. Soderstrom; are you satisfied? Having reduced my bright ideals to the cheapest shoddy, do you feel adequately revenged on me? Or on independent women?"

Soderstrom made a rough, impatient motion. "I don't care about that. I had something else in mind. I—"

"But you don't like independent women," Hannah persisted,

plainly antagonized now and unwilling to let the matter pass lightly.

"Their independence, no." He frowned, abruptly knocked out his pipe on the callused heel of his palm. "I will not pretend. A man has his place, a woman hers. The order is there for a reason in nature, and not to be lightly upset. Maybe it will happen just so, like you told me once, but I can see bad coming out of it."

"But only bad? That is part of any change—the pain—but only that?" Without waiting for a reply, she said quickly, wonderingly, "I hadn't expected any of this of you."

"What?"

"The—the depth. The understanding. You are not gentle about it, but it's there."

"I am a rough man. I live rough and talk rough. That is my way. Part of it, I never learned English too good. But more, I never talk much. To feel, to think, to be alive—this is the real sense of things for me. I am stubborn, though."

"Yes, you're stubborn. And you don't want people to see another side of you. But why? Even your daughter—"

"Thera knows me, and there is no need for talk. Listen." He paused; he did not want to speak of these things, but this once he would, extracting the memories like infected teeth—maybe this was needed. "In Sweden, in our district, my family was important. We had land and money. But I had an older brother. In the old country, the oldest son inherits all. The other children must depend on his good will. Well, when our *for* died, we quarreled, me and my brother Tomaas, and he turned me out. This is hard, to have much and then nothing at all. I came to America, maybe looking for something. I got married, built up my farm, and by thirty, was on my way to being a big man in the county. Then many things. Hedda died. Then the crops . . . the locusts . . . the hail . . . drought. Year after year. If a man is what he feels, then I could not have been brought any lower. There was mills, there was lumber camps to work in, but I could not. I needed to stand as a man on my own feet, on my own land. This, and the need to start over, brought me out here."

"Pride," Hannah said softly, "and the land. I can understand that."

"Loftus Buckmaster's daughter should."

To this, she seemed on the verge of saying something sharp, but did not. After a moment she said obliquely, "You said before that you were not baiting me about my father . . . that you had something else in mind. What was it?"

I don't know, Soderstrom thought, but all the same, as if the words were forming of their own accord, he said suddenly, "I was not trying to hurt you. I was shooting in the dark, trying to say things I felt were true about you. I wanted to know for sure."

"But why should you care to know my private thoughts? I don't—"

"A man should know such things about a woman if he asks her to marry him."

The thing was out now, the last words he had ever expected to say again, least of all to such a woman as Hannah Kingery. Yet now they were out, it became suddenly as clear as breaking sunlight that he had been leading up to this all along, and even the reason why. So that he was ready when she said almost timidly, "Why"—she cleared her throat—"why do you want to marry me?"

"Good reasons. You need a man, I need a woman. You are strong and healthy, as a woman should be."

"Getting a wife is not like buying a—a brood mare, Mr. Soderstrom! I might have expected—"

"You will let me finish, missus, eh?" Soderstrom half-smiled. "You have spirit and courage, a woman alone and unarmed coming to warn me across country you didn't know so well that you didn't get yourself lost. That was a brave thing to do. You have the good feeling for the land, too. I would not have a woman without it. There are many things I could say, but what is talk? Do you want to hear them?"

"That won't be necessary." There might have been a faint tremor in her voice. "Because I won't marry you."

"Will you say why? Maybe it's that I am rough?"

Hannah said quietly, "Do you think I mind that? I grew up in a family of men, and Pa and Garth have about four years of

102

schooling between them. Chad and I only six years apiece. As for hardship, I knew little else with Dan."

"Then what?"

"I'm afraid of you, I suppose. Of the things I see in you and what they might lead you to do. I made a mistake in marrying a man totally unlike my father, but that mistake could work in reverse. Thank you, but no."

Soderstrom's brows drew together. "A man is good to egg on, even give money to, when he stands up to your pa. But for the same reasons, he is not good enough to marry, eh?"

Hannah said in some confusion, "I don't mean—well, certainly—it doesn't follow that those qualities are what I want in a husband."

"Is that all?" he asked coldly.

"I'm not sure, since it hasn't been mentioned, but does love enter into your scheme of what a marriage should be?"

That brought him up short. There had been only one woman in his life, and in most ways she had been little like Hannah Kingery. There had been no sparring of complex thoughts and words with Hedda, only a good understanding, direct and simple and intense, that was unmistakably what men and women called love. "I know this much," he said finally, slowly. "I need a wife. Love I had once. Maybe it could be again, maybe in time. I can't say for sure. It could be good, even so." He paused. "If it were not for the other thing, I wonder . . . would you take the chance?"

"I—I can't answer that. I've had much of the romance knocked out of me, as I'm sure is the case with you. Perhaps to the good—perhaps people would be better off by being realistic. By hoping, at the most, to make a good life together." She looked away, then looked back at him as if on swift impulse. "Is there any gentleness in you? Will you ever show me that you can be gentle?"

"That is a hell of a question, woman."

"Your actions will answer it," she said quietly. "Please, let's don't talk any more about this. Can't we walk back now?"

Twelve

Chad Buckmaster tied his horse to the edge of the cottonwood motte after a careless glance at the circling hills, then strolled through the trees and down the creekbank. Halting by the water's edge, he dropped to his haunches beneath the mottling of leaf shadow and amused himself by breaking twigs in small pieces and tossing them at skittering waterbugs. While he waited for his brother's wife.

Almost idly, he wondered about that. Naomi was pretty enough, not very smart, docile and willing, with all the direct passion of a simple woman. This was pleasant frosting, but the cake itself, he supposed, was his big brother and the dominating shadow he had always cast across Chadwick's life.

Chad could not remember when it had been otherwise. Garth had been the firstborn son, the image of his father, and from the first, the old man had pinned his hopes for an earthly immortality (Loftus believed in no other sort) on Garth. When, as both boys grew older, it had become apparent that Garth was a dull-headed brute, the old man had stubbornly refused to relinquish that early hope, though it was equally clear that Chad was the heir to his father's wit and shrewdness.

At times Chad plunged with a will into the business of keeping the gears of Wagontree oiled and smooth-running; his Buckmaster's pride was deep and genuine, and not to be denied. But usually a growing bitter indifference was uppermost; the game did not seem worth the candle, and idleness and liquor and women were useful for dulling the knowledge.

There was nothing obscure about the satisfaction of dalliance with his brother's wife; it temporarily gave him a kind of rancid ascendancy over Garth, but did nothing to solve his larger dilemma.

Hearing a slow beat of hooves now, he rose off his haunches and peered through the trees with the lazy thought that perhaps he should be more careful. But it was Naomi, all right, and she stepped to the ground and left her horse, coming quickly to him. Her lips held a wild eagerness, and she trembled in his arms; he looked over her head with a wry and crooked grin.

"What's the matter?"

"It's all this . . . sneaking about, I guess. Hannah paid a visit yesterday."

"So Pa mentioned to me."

"But, Chad, she knows about us. She told me she saw us here together."

Chad scowled, but only shrugged after a moment. "So? If she was going to tell anyone else, she would have by now. What are you worried about?"

"If she could find out, so can others." She pressed tightly against his chest, shuddering. "I'm afraid. If we could only leave here. . . . Chad?"

"It's no good," he said patiently. "I told you before, once I leave Wagontree, I'm nothing."

She drew back slowly, looking at his face. "What are you here, Chad? What is either of us?"

Chad thumbed his hat back off his sweat-damp curls, thinking wryly. *Christ, every time she's been talking to Han, you see sudden courage. That will last about a week.* "Fed and sheltered, with every comfort. I don't aim to give that up. Neither do you, if you think a while."

"And Garth would follow us . . . of course?"

"That's right."

"Hannah thought that you'd told me that," Naomi murmured. "She said something else, too. That you were lying when you said you loved me."

Chad said feelingly, "Hell," with a wash of unfeigned irritation. "That damned meddler. Sure I love you. Who do you believe, anyway?"

"I told her I believed you."

105

"That answers it for everyone," Chad said softly. "Come here. Come here now." She whispered his name blindly and came against him, and her response was fierce and breathless.

A sharp crackle of brush high along the bank several yards down yanked Chad alert. He half-turned; he pushed Naomi away in the same instant that the huge, bullish form of his brother broke from a clot of thickets. Garth roared something inarticulate, and his gun came up.

There was no time to think. Chad's reaction was purely instinctive, letting reflex dip his hand down and up: his gunbutt slapped snug against his palm and the barrel came up in a lifting sideward arc. He had a glimpse of Garth's wide dark face before the roar of the two guns merged.

Garth was jolted back as if by a giant fist, and his knees folded. He fell over the cutbank and skidded down its crumbling slant till his face and one arm rested in the water.

Chad took two steps forward, dumbly holding his gun pointed out. Then he halted, letting his fist drop. There was an acid taste in his mouth as the brutal and inescapable fact of what had happened sank home.

Somehow Garth's suspicions had become aroused enough for him to follow one or the other of them today, but what did that matter? *Garth is dead. He's dead. Now what will you do? It was self-defense, wasn't it?* Quite abruptly, his mind was cold and clear. *Maybe that's good enough, but maybe not. A story is no better than it sounds. You killed your brother because he tried to kill you for stealing his wife. How will that sound to a cow country jury? But suppose you could satisfy the law; what about Pa? Garth was his pride and joy. He'll have your scalp one way or the other.*

His hand, as he rubbed it over his mouth, was shaking, and he held it out and halted his thoughts until it stopped shaking. He thought, *Now that's better,* and looked down at Naomi. She had dropped to her knees, hands flat to her cheeks, making small half-hysterical sounds. He could not tell whether she was trying to retch or moan.

"What will we do, Chad?" she whimpered, and without waiting for an answer, "I . . . I . . . I'm going to be sick."

Chad said, "All right, be sick," and climbed the bank in

lunging steps. He searched through the grove till he found Garth's big black, tied in a tangle of young willows.

Even as he reached for the animal's halter, the solution came with a hard, savage certainty. By now half the people in Buckmaster County knew that Garth and Krag Soderstrom had fought, and that Garth had taken the first whipping of his life while barely getting a hand on the Swede. Garth had not been shy about proclaiming his intent to somehow retaliate.

Chad thought with a quiet exultance, *It will work out fine.* And it would swing suspicion away from him beyond any doubt. He let the thought pause, backtracking: *What about Naomi?* Then he smiled, certain of his ability to handle her. He was still smiling as he pushed back through the grove toward the creekbank, leading Garth's black.

Today's drive had been held to an easy pace, and Soderstrom called an early halt not far from Baxley's Peak. He made his plan with deliberate care, consulting Rafe Catron's knowledge of the country. He had, Soderstrom said grimly, lost his other herd because the lay of the land had worked against him; this time it would fall to his advantage.

They made camp in a long valley enclosed by two well-timbered ridges, with a narrow pass at each end. To any watcher on the dark ridges above, the bedgrounds and fire-light camp and scattered gear and small remuda picketed nearby would present the ordinary activity of any trail camp settled down for the night.

Soderstrom assigned Waco Millard, who was no hand with a gun and who would probably cut a sorry figure in any fight, to the first nighthawk shift. The herd was still behaving well, having been eased along as always, and the long valley contained a good spring and plenty of grass. If any commotion did spook them slightly, the ridges and Waco's guard should hold them all right.

Soderstrom yawned elaborately, tossed the dregs of his coffee into the fire, and reached for his bedroll. Rafe and McIver followed his example, not hurrying about it. Soderstrom stretched out and folded his arms under his head and looked at the stars, fighting the tug of drowsiness.

By tomorrow night, if all went well, the herd would be deep inside the county and Otis Crashaw's jurisdiction; and he would have won a victory that would at once begin to diminish the legend that was Loftus Buckmaster. For Loftus had cast his whole game on tonight's fall of the dice, and already his plan was betrayed, the game half-lost. *It is too bad,* Soderstrom thought, *but you asked for this, old man, and Soderstrom is obliging.*

Still, he felt a restlessness and discomfort, dispelling the temptation of sleep. Hannah Kingery had stayed over the night before at the Blue Springs camp, setting out early the next morning for Mimbreno. Their parting had been brief and unsatisfactory, and thinking back on this, and on her quiet and emphatic turndown of his proposal, words he had spoken to only one other woman in his life, Soderstrom felt angry and unhappy.

He could not salve his pride by deceiving himself, being a deep and stolid man who did not take such things lightly, that he had proposed on an impulse prompted by infatuation which he might well have regretted later. The thing had been slowly building all along, and had bided its time until the moment of realization. He had thought about it through the long day, and he could not give himself the lie; it had been this way only once before, with Hedda, and the fact that this time the knowledge had come with great reluctance, little by little, made it no less certain. *Be gentle* ... what did a woman expect of a man?

The fire had died to red coals, and their tawny glow began to fade. When he was sure that the presumed watcher above could no longer make out their blanketed forms, Soderstrom stirred upright in his blankets and reached an arm to shake McIver, who likewise roused Rafe.

Picking up their rifles, the three men moved with a stealthy care through the windless darkness toward the north end of the valley with its boulder-flanked pass. A sliver of moon shed the faintest light and whitened the boulders enough to silhouette any moving dark object.

They took their positions, Soderstrom on one side close to the outer mouth of the pass, McIver and Rafe stationed farther back on opposite flanks. With each man laid up behind a boulder, they had only to wait.

It seemed a long time. Soderstrom began to sweat at each fancied sound. Finally came the clop of muffled hooves, and he saw them ride slowly out of a black swatch of timber—three, five, six riders altogether. They would, he guessed, simply adapt their old tactic to the present circumstances. Beyond to the south of the valley lay a region of shattered volcanic rock, of which the herders had made a wide skirt today. There was no cliff to dynamite, but a sudden yelling charge might just as effectively stampede the cattle through the south pass and into death.

Soderstrom's heart pounded against the cool boulder. When he judged they were close enough, he drew in his breath, and rapped out: "Throw up your hands!"

The warning would give justification to what, he saw almost at once, could not be avoided. There was a hoarse shout as a rider spurred forward. Soderstrom shot the man from his saddle. Rafe and McIver fired together, and a second man tumbled from his horse and was dragged by a stirruped foot as it wheeled, bolting.

For Soderstrom, the rest was a pandemonium of wild yells, gunfire, and the stink of burned powder. The raiders dismounted and scattered for cover, and there was no certain target except illusive shadows and stabs of gunflame. Soderstrom became aware that he was levering an empty rifle, and the barrel was so hot he could hardly hold it. He shrank down against his rock and fumbled for fresh cartridges.

A sudden pound of hooves pulled his head up, and he had time only to see the rider, hanging low on his horse's side, veer recklessly down on him. He was not sure afterward whether the man leaped from his saddle or whether he dragged him off. He heard the man's pistol hammer fall on a spent shell, and then they were rolling and tussling across the stony ground.

His adversary was slight, but wiry as a weasel, and Soderstrom had his hands full. He saw faint light glance off a knifeblade and grabbed desperately for an unseen wrist and got it. For an instant, under the moonlight, he caught the grimacing face of Richie Sears. Then he recoiled from the pain of a knee close to his groin, and they broke apart.

The din of shots filled Soderstrom's ears as he scrambled to his knees. Sears was already on his feet and his dim form was weaving in low and fast, the knife poised. Coming up off his knees, not wholly on his feet, Soderstrom dove beneath the raised knife and butted Sears in the stomach. He heard a gush of breath and the deflected knifethrust ripped his shirt and grazed coldly along his ribs. Soderstrom gave a savage heave of his shoulder, his feet still driving, and Sears went down and Soderstrom fell on him and half-pinned him. Sears got an arm free and swung the knife back for another try. Soderstrom smashed his fist against the gunman's wrist and the knife clattered into the rocks.

His hold was poor, and Sears, writhing like a snake, broke away. Anticipating him, Soderstrom went after the knife on his hands and knees and got it and came around on his knees. He saw Sears almost on top of him, swinging a good-sized rock. Soderstrom thrust upward with the knife, a clumsy underhand stab. The point took Sears' raised arm at the elbow and tore upward through cloth and flesh.

The gunman pulled back and came to his feet, holding his arm. He made no sound, but Soderstrom knew the razor-edged steel had cut deeply. The gunfire had slackened off, and Soderstrom called hoarsely, "All right, quit."

"You better finish this, snork."

Soderstrom still palmed the bloody knife and breathing deeply now, he lowered it. He could not see Sears' face; his low, shaken words told enough. The shooting had stopped. Soderstrom saw in the thin moonlight that both Rafe and McIver were unhit, and were holding their guns on the three living raiders. One man was squatting down, cuddling a wounded arm. Two men lay dark and crumpled and still on the pale canyon floor. Soderstrom herded Sears over with the others, then retrieved his rifle. Methodically, he reloaded the magazine, and tramped over beside Rafe Catron.

"We got 'em tighter than a flea's ass," Rafe exulted with a wolfish satisfaction. "This time we can string up the lot."

Soderstrom shuttled a speculative glance at him. "That's a far tune from what you was singing, mister."

"Hell, this time we got 'em tight. No twelve men in cow country would give you one day for hanging the bastards."

Soderstrom smiled grimly. So much of your fine goodness in people boiled down to exactly this: Never cut a man's throat till it seems a safe thing to do. He said to Sears, "No Buckmaster is along?"

"Garth was supposed to lead this party," Sears husked. "He went somewhere this morning and wasn't about when we left. The old man sent Chad out with some men to find him. You better do it like that redneck said, snork, and finish this with a rope."

Unwillingly, Soderstrom was hearing Hannah's words again: *Show me that you can be gentle;* and now he said coldly, half-absently, "Why?"

"I think you ruint my arm for good." Sears' breathing was labored and broken. "You better finish this. You better, snork, or you're dead."

"Now I'm worried," Soderstrom said. "Anyway, this will be the third time for you, and they say that works the charm."

"Third time I what?"

"That you made a long walk home. If these others don't know how, you can show them."

Thirteen

Soderstrom made the two unhurt raiders bury their dead companions where they had fallen. They worked half the night, wresting huge chunks of rock out of two deep holes in the stony soil. A gunmetal hint of dawn had tinged the east when they finished piling up the cairns of heavy boulders over each grave. Afterward they, with Sears and the other

111

wounded man, were turned loose, unarmed, to find their way back afoot to Wagontree where Loftus Buckmaster would be waiting word of their success. Soderstrom told Rafe Catron to drive their mounts away in the opposite direction and abandon them.

Rafe did as he was told and said nothing, but he was nursing a bitter anger. He had only to touch the ugly scar on his throat to remember, with shuddering clarity, that morning when Wagontree men had strung him up with no concern for his innocence or guilt. All right, he'd admittedly known that the steer was a Wagontree animal even before the hair had been clipped from the incriminating brand—a point he glossed over whenever he repeated the story—nor had that been the only strange beef to feel his butchering knife or branding iron over the last several years.

Still, just as his own guilt or innocence meant nothing to big augurs like the Buckmasters, so Rafe did not view any act committed against their kind as theft, but only simple justice. Rafe needed the taste of wild freedom as some men needed whiskey or women or good food, but times were mostly hard for any loner, and having no respect for society, he felt no scruples about easing his situation at society's expense. There was, particularly, a downright pleasure in taking from big, bloated augurs like the Buckmasters, who had built fortunes out of running roughshod over the little man.

Since the hanging that had failed, his hatred for them had deepened to a passion, but it went back a good deal further. . . .

After scattering the raiders' horses, Rafe returned to the camp, where Waco and McIver were huddled by the fire in the chill gray dawn, watching coffee come to a boil.

"Where's Soderstrom, Mac?"

"Out on nighthawk," McIver replied. "He says to get a couple hours' rest; we'll be moving out early."

Rafe squatted on his heels and rolled a twisted thin cigar between his teeth, reaching for a burning twig. "We shouldn't of let 'em off. I can't figure him."

"We're in Addison County," McIver pointed out. "The county

seat is two hundred miles away. We'd be days getting them there, even if we hadn't a herd on our hands."

Waco gave a shrill whistle of a laugh. "Youngster, Rafe wasn't meaning that just exactly. No, sir."

Rafe grunted, tossing the twig back in the fire. "My pappy used to say, always eat your bird in the hand."

"You must think a great deal of your father," McIver said.

"Thought. He's dead." Rafe stood abruptly, walking off a few steps. He watched the dawn grow and puffed his cigarette, feeling the chill pain of memory. It seemed closer and sharper on this cold morning than it had in years, and he knew this was because he was brooding about matters that couldn't be helped. Still, he found himself remembering.

Like hundreds of Texans returning to their homes after the War between the states, Sol Catron, Rafe's father, had found a broken, impoverished land with only one natural resource: countless thousands of longhorn cattle running wild in the brush. Sol had gradually built up his herd and, after a few trail drives to Galveston, had restored his family to a decent life. But fresh prosperity had attracted a loose confederation of rustler bands who moved stolen stock in night drives down to crooked buyers on the Gulf Coast. It was an "underground" operation, secret and well-organized. Inevitably, since a man's closest neighbor might be a cog in the crooked machinery, some innocent men fell under suspicion. A man like Sol Catron, taciturn and noted for his lonesome ways, made a natural suspect.

A semi-vigilante group headed by a blood-hungry sheriff in the pay of the big ranchers was drafted to deal with the situation. One night they had ridden up to Sol Catron's home and called his name. When he stepped into the yard, he was riddled by a score of bullets. Rafe and his mother were ordered out then, and every building on the place fired.

In Rafe Catron's mind, The Law was a powerful tool that wore the mask of justice and, in practice, was for sale to the top bidder. He hated The Law, but he feared it, too, and fear had bred a dim respect for its cold, malleable processes. Only a fool threw himself head-on against it, but by the same token only a fool did not get away with whatever he safely could when the opportunity afforded itself. . . .

The drive resumed at full dawn, though the night's broken pattern had meant little sleep for any of them. Soderstrom was impatient to see his herd safe across the county line. Rafe's spirits rose somewhat with the climbing sun. Last night's business had been, after all, a handy piece of work, and he felt vindicated in his decision of weeks ago to tie his star to Soderstrom's. The Swede was a fighter; he had brains and guts and tenacity, and these were paying off fat dividends on Rafe's old score with the Buckmasters. A contented grin cracked his dusty jaw; all that was lacking was a sight of old Loftus' face when he learned about last night.

Midday crept into deep afternoon, and they were perhaps five miles into Buckmaster County when a lone rider came up from the southeast, bearing directly for them. Soderstrom's keen eyes were the first to note the horseman, and he ordered a halt. The last stragglers were milling to a stop as Sheriff Crashaw rode up to Soderstrom and Rafe dropped over to that flank to catch the exchange between them.

"I want you to come in with me till this is cleared up," Crashaw was saying.

Soderstrom's face held a fierce bleakness, and he glanced at Rafe as he rode up. "Here's Catron. He'll tell you I have not been out of his sight in many days. So will McIver and Millard."

"What is this?" Rafe demanded.

"Garth Buckmaster is missing since early yesterday," Soderstrom said tersely. "It is remembered that I said I'd kill him if he ever set foot on my land. Now his horse has been found killed by a bullet, deep on our south range."

"Found by who?" Rafe's voice was parched and cracked. "When?"

"This noon," Crashaw said. "By Chad Buckmaster and three Wagontree hands who been on the search for Garth since yesterday."

Rafe turned a taut, furious glance on the sheriff. "But hellfire! You can't hang this on the boss. It's like he said, we all been close to him every minute since we picked up this herd."

"Maybe," Soderstrom said gently, "the sheriff thinks you would all lie for the boss, eh?"

Crashaw shook his head. "No accusation. We don't even know what, if anything, happened to Garth. There's still some pointed facts here that can't be brushed away. One, you made a threat against Garth's life in front of witnesses. Two, you said if he ever set foot on your land, and that's where we found his horse. Three, the black was shot dead by someone, suggesting that Garth himself might of run into something similar."

Surprisingly, Soderstrom smiled. "How long was the horse dead?"

"Since early yesterday, Chad reckoned."

"Early yesterday, I was a good twenty miles from here. You think, then, I left my trail herd that I was driving short-handed to ride home and kill Garth Buckmaster because I knew—God knows how—I would find him on my land?" Soderstrom paused sardonically. "That would be quite a trick, Sheriff, even if my three men would all lie for me. Even if you had a body, which you admit you don't, except his horse's, eh?"

Crashaw was unruffled. "I'll find out the rest soon enough. All right, you have an alibi, and I don't even have a warrant. You're a hard-nosed citizen, Soderstrom, but I think you're an honest one. You'd want to abide by the law, even go off your way to help it if you could."

"I don't understand you, mister."

"After Chad told his pa about finding Garth's horse, the old man sent a hand to fetch me. I came fast, because I know Loftus Buckmaster as well as I do. He never had more ado with law or courts than he needed to, and a man his age has got deep habits. He minded what I told him and you, too, so he had me fetched, but what's holding him back from acting on his own makes a damn thin halter. He ain't going to bother with the sense of it: if something's happened to his boy, someone has got to pay, and that'll just naturally be the man who beat him up and threatened him. You."

Crashaw paused, then went on, "But here's the thing: he ain't sure yet, not without he knows what happened to Garth. When I asked him to give me time to find out what happened, he agreed, but on condition. He is afraid that if you done for Garth, you'll sneak away meantime. If I put you safely behind bars till I turn something up, I can keep Loftus simmered down. Otherwise he won't give his word to hold in. He made no bones about saying so.

"Now see where this has to lead? I can't hold him back alone, and men'll be killed. I don't want that, and I don't think you do."

Soderstrom considered for a moment, then nodded. "All right. I will go to Mimbreno and be locked up."

Rafe made a bitter objection, but Soderstrom said, "It must be this way. Right or wrong, I have respect for the law. And this is the best way to show my innocence. Now, we'll bed the cattle and eat, and the sheriff and me will ride to Mimbreno before dark."

"Good," Crashaw said. "Loftus warned he'd send a man into town tonight to check my lockup and make sure you was there."

Camp was made in a jag of cottonwoods bordering a sallow trickle of creek, and Soderstrom went over the sheriff's story with him several times, talking calmly and quietly. But Rafe had no stomach for food or talk; what had really happened was clear enough to him, and the conviction was balling like sour curd in his belly.

As soon as they had eaten, Soderstrom left with Crashaw, his parting order to Rafe being simply for Rafe to drive the shorthorns onto Ladder and scatter them, ending their potential as a target. For some minutes after he was gone, Rafe sat in silence, brooding sullenly at the fire. Only he and Waco Millard were in camp, McIver having taken the first night-hawk watch at the herd bedgrounds a quarter mile away. Waco sat cross-legged across the fire, watching Rafe suck cigarette after cigarette down to a stub, and his seamed face held a searching caution. Finally he said, tentatively, "If Garth turns up dead Soderstrom will be in real trouble, hunh?"

"Dead, hell!" Rafe's raw throat gave his voice a rasp, and he pitched his cigarette in the fire. "You jughead, don't you understand what that old devil Loftus has done? What he done was have Garth's horse hazed over onto Ladder and shot. Then Garth himself will lay low for a spell. Weeks maybe, or months. As long as the old man wants Soderstrom in jail and out of the way. Anyway it goes, Buckmaster has time to size up his next move."

Waco was utterly silent, unmoving on his haunches, as he digested this. Then he said in a voice of hate, "Looks like them bastards have taken the prize, Rafe."

Rafe looked blindly at the fire, unwilling to accept the situation. *Right or wrong,* Soderstrom had said, *I have respect for the law.* That was Soderstrom, but how could Rafe Catron, hating the law, swallow this savage injustice?

And then, as an idea took seed, he thought, *Maybe a frame-up can work two ways.* The details began crowding him thick and fast, so that he stood and paced back and forth in his excitement. Suddenly he swung to face Waco. "Last night the Buckmasters tried for us outside Crashaw's territory. What if they tried again tonight?"

Waco waggled his white head. "They won't, not and draw Crashaw's fire."

Rafe said softly, "Suppose they did, though. Suppose that twenty, thirty head of our shorthorns was killed by night riders and you or me could say positive that Chad Buckmaster was the leader?"

Waco's scarred face twitched as understanding came. "That would settle one Buckmaster's hash for certain-sure. Go a long way toward settling this child's old score, too."

Rafe nodded, knowing that he had a fast ally in Waco, whose hatred for the Buckmasters outmatched his own. "There's Natchez Canyon two miles over east of here. If a bunch of cattle hit that rim in a solid run, you could write them off to a critter."

"Only there's McIver." Waco's expression drained from his face and left it a blank mask. "I don't allow he'd go along, Rafe."

117

"No," Rafe said slowly. "The two of us can handle it, but we got to make it look right to Mac."

They talked the plan over for a half-hour, refining it here and there, until Rafe was satisfied that it rang about as true as human wit could contrive. When McIver's watch was ended, he would come in and wake Rafe for his stint. Rafe would ride out his two-hour watch, then Waco would join him and they would do the job quickly. The racket would wake McIver, but too late for him to suspect the truth. The story they would give him, and later Sheriff Crashaw, was that there had been a surprise attack by perhaps five or so night riders, who came down yelling and shooting and got behind an isolated bunch of shorthorns and ran it off. They had tried to make a stand, but were forced to retreat from superior numbers. However, they had identified the voice of the man calling the orders as Chad Buckmaster's. Then, having done their work, the raiders had vanished in the night.

Tonight, when McIver rode in off watch, both men were snoring in their blankets. Actually Rafe was awake and restless, but after McIver had shaken him awake, he made a show of stumbling groggily over to the picket line, lugging his saddle.

After two hours of watch, he was joined by Waco. Almost without words they went quickly to work, aided by the thin moonlight. The first part was the hardest, quietly cutting out twenty head from the flank of the herd. Afterward the two men hazed the smaller bunch off east, slowly so as not to alarm the herd.

A good half-mile from the main herd, Rafe pulled his gun and fired into the air. It was the signal, and now Waco joined him, firing, punctuating the shots with wild yells. The bunch shifted into a nervous trot, getting momentum. Shortly, lengthened into a loose wedge, they broke into a full stampede.

The bunch poured onto the east flat in a rumbling dark stream, and ahead now Rafe spotted the jagged form of dark boulders against the skyline. It marked the rim of the canyon, and he bawled at the top of his voice for Waco to stretch out and flank the running brutes. The bunch must be pointed into a shallow cleft which formed a natural trail to the very brink of the canyon.

Rafe and Waco pulled back off flank as the dark wedge hit the broad mouth of the cleft at a hurtling run. Then the lifting shoulders of rock, tapering inward, compressed it without slowing its doomed momentum.

The leaders neared the rim and tried to stop, and then the surging juggernaut behind them pushed them over. A slow milling began as the drag came up against the first resistance. The two men hoorawed the panicked animals relentlessly on, and Rafe could make out the dark bobbing humps skylined on the rim as they made the plunge.

Only a few head managed the last-minute turn and broke back past the men to safety. An almost invisible haze of dust made the night acrid as Rafe sidled his mount cautiously over to the rim and looked down. The bawling of crippled and dying cattle rose in a vast chorus of misery from the darkness below.

Rafe was a cowman born and raised, and all his instincts shriveled in protest against the total and savage wantonness of his own action. He said harshly, "Come on," and swung back from the rim. Waco followed him silently.

Before they had gone a dozen yards, Rafe had the shock of seeing a horse and rider lift suddenly out of the darkness. The horse was slowed to a trot, but it was winded and blowing, and his mind had barely registered this fact before McIver's flat question came.

"Night riders, Mac," Rafe fumbled. "Eh, we tried to stop 'em—"

"Both of you?"

"Well, I had just rousted Waco out for his watch when the two of us heard something out there. So we rode back together to see what, and got to the herd just as all hell busted loose."

McIver said with a cool, baffled anger, "That's a lie. Waco was restless, and that brought me awake. He was acting in a peculiar way, so I pretended to be still asleep. And I saw him ride out alone. I saddled up and followed him, but I was too far behind. But I know what you did, Rafe, and I can guess why."

A thick dread tightened Rafe's belly, and he said softly, "That 'why' ought to make a difference, Mac."

McIver shook his head curtly. "It doesn't. Don't waste your breath, Rafe. In the morning we'll ride in to see the sheriff. You'll tell him and Soderstrom exactly what you've done—or I will."

Rafe said sharply, "Mac, wait," as McIver turned his horse away, riding off. His shoulders and head made a faint outline as he topped a slant in the trail, and in that moment, Waco cocked his pistol. The sound washed against Rafe's brain like a dash of ice water, and he drove a heel into his horse's flank, lunging the animal sideward into Waco's mount as the gun roared.

He heard McIver's strained grunt of pain, and then McIver kicked his horse forward into a run, bowed across its mane, and in an instant was gone over the rise. Waco was fighting for control of his prancing horse, and he shrilled, "You crazy? Why he—"

Rafe cursed him, and heeled his horse into motion and went up over the rise and down its far side. The gully was banked with dense shadow, and he moved down it cautiously. Then he saw McIver's riderless horse.

Rafe stepped down and stooped low and struck a match. The washback of light showed dark wet stains on the rocks. He followed them up the stony bank to where they faded out in a vast litter of boulders. McIver must have been jolted from his saddle, but he had had enough left to push off on foot. The match burned Rafe's fingers and he struck another and studied the ground, feeling the hammerbeat of his pulse. There was nothing, and now he listened for a sound. There was none. McIver had faded into the forest of rock, and there would be no finding him in the dark. He was hard-hit, perhaps dying, but he might still stay on his feet a long while.

Rafe dropped the match, his mouth dry. Suddenly things had gotten out of hand in a way he had not foreseen, and he was in far above his head. A suffocating fear came over him, and on its heels the cold alternatives—*run or bluff it through?* McIver might live to talk, but alone and losing blood, he might be dead before morning. Rafe reached for a blind courage now, and, beyond that, did not allow himself to think. He climbed heavily down the bank to get his horse, and already he was revising his story for the sheriff and Soderstrom.

Fourteen

After the set fashion of an aging man, Otis Crashaw greeted each day according to a strict and unvarying ritual. He rose directly at 6:00, went into the kitchen, started his fire, filled the coffeepot, and laid strips of bacon in the frying pan. He washed up and honed his ancient razor, paused to turn over the bacon, then shaved with short, careful strokes. At 6:20 he broke two eggs into the spitting bacon grease, then dressed himself. He ate unhurriedly and fired up his pipe. He locked his front door at exactly 6:54 and made a leisurely stroll uptown to his office and the day's duties.

Crashaw liked the comfortable routine of his life of the last several years. He had often congratulated himself on buying his little house on the edge of town. It was a refuge where a man could enjoy a quiet pipe after a long day and muse on the past. Being sheriff of a finely populated county in a backwater of a dying frontier placed few demands on his waning energies. Loftus Buckmaster had brought him here, but the little people had voted him in, proud that a great marshal of the boomtown days had chosen to cap a turbulent life by making his home among them.

Lately Otis Crashaw had given much thought to what he owed these people. Too many years in a line of work that was brutal and often dirty had blunted his conscience to a dry cynicism. As his eye and hand had slowed down, he had become satisfied to take with both hands whatever past-earned glory might get him and ask few questions. But the recent choice he'd made had sharpened his blunted tools and tempered them with a new outlook. At sixty-three he had begun to find meaning in work he had always followed because it suited him.

As always, he found the street deserted at this early hour. The sky, he noticed, had a faint bleak overcast, and he sniffed the air and decided that a heller of a storm would hit before long. He might have to postpone the search for Garth Buckmaster for a while, no bad prospect if the Swede were a good checkers player.

Nearing the office he felt a nudge of curiosity at the sight of a rider coming into town from the north, moving briskly. Recognizing Rafe Catron then, Crashaw quickened his steps and reached the tie rail by his office as Rafe stepped down. Catron was usually a loafer and ne'er-do-well and, Crashaw was reasonably sure, a petty cow thief of long standing, but too trifling and easy-going to take very seriously. So Crashaw's greeting was neutral and mildly curious.

"It'll take some telling," Rafe said soberly, and tilted his head toward the jail. "Reckon the boss had better hear this, too, if he's in there."

Crashaw unlocked his office. The jail comprised two large cells with steel-barred doors at the rear of the room. In one of these, Krag Soderstrom was stretched out on the bunk, wide awake, hands folded behind his neck. He came to his feet in one complete motion, reminding Crashaw of a large, powerful cat.

"Bunk hard enough for you?"

"I slept on groundsheets softer," Soderstrom said, walking to the barred door. "Well, Catron, you moved the herd home already?"

"Not yet." Rafe removed his hat, cuffing the dust from it. "There was trouble last night. Wagontree raided again. Reckon they want to take advantage of the herd being still bunched."

Crashaw glanced at Soderstrom, and the Swede's eyes seemed to burn deeply as he said, "Go on."

"They was at least ten. If we hadn't made a game fight, they would of got off with the whole herd. As it was, they managed to drive a good twenty or more head off the edge of

Natchez Canyon. We looked down there this morning." Catron shook his head, dropping his gaze to his hat. "Worst of it, Mac is missing. He was shot and his horse bolted. After it was over, I looked for him. Couldn't make out in the dark. Searched awhile after it turned light enough, and kept Waco looking while I come in to tell you and the sheriff. Figured you'd want to know at once."

"All right," Crashaw said with a weary bafflement. "You know they was Wagontree men?"

"Sure. Both me and Waco recognized Chad Buckmaster's voice. He give the orders. Don't offhand know of any other outfit he rides with, do you?"

Soderstrom spoke now, with a contained and wicked anger. "All right, Sheriff, I'm taking you at your word. Is your jail big enough to hold Chad Buckmaster?"

Crashaw was troubled. There was much in this situation that did not tongue-and-groove cleanly, and he did not like it. He had made his own position clear to Loftus Buckmaster, and was sure that he had left Buckmaster with no doubts of the consequences of any move against the Swede in this county. He said slowly, "It makes no sense. Loftus knows when not to spit in a man's eye."

Soderstrom said flatly, "A man can get desperate, being kingpin so long and watching it slip away."

"Maybe. I'll tell you this: Catron and Millard better be sure."

Rafe shifted his feet. "Would swear to it on my pappy's grave. Waco, too."

Crashaw nodded tiredly. "I'll get a warrant and ride out to Wagontree. The warrant will only get Chad."

Soderstrom frowned, chewing his mustache. "Maybe you should take along a pair of special deputies. Catron and me."

"No." Crashaw shook his head. "That would make trouble for sure. I don't understand all that's going on, but one thing for sure about old Loftus: he coppers all bets. If Chad was with that bunch last night, any number of lying witnesses have been primed with his alibi. Chad was playing cards with the boys in the bunkhouse half the night, or he was pulling taffy with his daddy. He'll have no reason not to come peaceably."

"Wait." Soderstrom gripped the bars in both hands. "Handle Buckmaster any way you want, but let me out now."

Crashaw had started for the door, and now he halted. "Why?"

"You heard Catron. McIver is bad hurt, maybe dying, somewhere out there. He is my man, and seeing after him is my job. I got to look for him."

"If he's dead," Crashaw said dryly, "it don't matter. If he was hurt bad, he didn't get far and your men can look for him in a tight area. If he still ain't found, then it becomes my job. Anyhow I want you right where you are, Soderstrom. I'll have enough of a time holding Buckmaster down without worrying about you, too."

A vein of temper swelled and beat in Soderstrom's temple, but he held his voice low. "You are wrong. I want to look after a man of mine. Not get revenge for those cattle. If it was otherwise, I would say so. That is my word."

"I won't take the chance." Crashaw's tone was hard with a growing irritation, and he thumbed Catron toward the door. "Outside, so I can lock up the place. I'm taking no chance with you, either."

Catron went silently out ahead of him, then stood watching Crashaw lock the door. "You worried I might try to bust him out?"

"Yes. There's your horse. Fork him and ride."

He waited till Catron had ridden out of sight, then went to the livery and ordered his horse saddled. Moments later, as he was jogging down the street, he saw Hannah Kingery and Soderstrom's daughter leave the newspaper building. Both girls were carrying covered trays, which meant they were heading for his office. Last night, when he had brought Soderstrom in, he had granted the Swede's request to see his daughter before being locked up. It had been agreed then that Hannah and Thera would prepare all of Soderstrom's meals.

Reining over to them now, Crashaw touched his hat. "Sorry, but the office is locked up." He explained why, uneasy under the cold resentment of Hannah Kingery's stare. Beneath the professional disdain he had cultivated toward them, women always made him uneasy. But the response of mingled shock and distress in the Soderstrom girl's face was harder to endure, and then he realized that worry for young McIver was the case. After a hesitation, he said gruffly, "Look, Missy. Window of your pa's cell opens off behind the building. You can talk to him back there, and pass his food through the bars."

Thera thanked him, but Hannah's silent and icy stare did not relax. *The hell with her,* Crashaw thought, as he rode toward the courthouse. After rousing the clerk who slept in a back room, he left with a warrant in his pocket.

It was early forenoon when he put his horse up the long west slope of the hill beyond which Wagontree headquarters sprawled. The place always put him in mind of the old-time monarchies he had read about. Bad thing about a monarchy was the hereditary part; a strong man assembled power in his lifetime, but like as not the blood ran thin in his heirs.

That thought was trivial. His mind had always veered to triviality when there was a danger that the real issue might impel fear. Crashaw, not being a fool, knew that gaunt specter of old. He wiped his hand along his pants to dry the perspiration, then looked at it. It was trembling. It always trembled now, even when he was not afraid. *Too old,* he thought bleakly; you could fight fear and even sickness, but not that.

Coming off the wagon road into the layout, Crashaw loosened his gun in its holster. His muscles were too tight for comfort, and he forced a slackness to them as he threaded through the outbuildings. The blacksmith shop was deserted as he passed it, but from the house, still out of sight, came a dog's excited barking, as if something were up. Crashaw rode unhurriedly to face whatever it was; the baffling events of the last few days, coupled by the strange disappearance of Garth Buckmaster, had left him wearily ready for anything.

Most of the Wagontree crew, he saw as he came into view of the house, was gathered in the yard. They were armed to a man, sitting their horses in a kind of deadly hush. Chad was one of them; he had reined in close to the veranda where his father stood, leaning heavily on a pair of crutches, as if the slightest movement cost him infinite agony. Crashaw's glance flicked to Naomi Buckmaster, who was leaning in the doorway looking on. Her face was deathly pale, he saw, and suddenly sensed the probable reason for this assembly of force.

Loftus had been speaking, and now he was letting his words sink in. Crashaw ranged up to the veranda steps, saying mildly, "What's this, Loftus?"

Loftus did not even look at him, and it was Chad who spoke. "Me and the boys found Garth's body on Ladder ground. It was buried on a ridge back of Soderstrom's house."

"You and the boys, huh? You knew directly where to look?"

"In a way," Chad said soberly. "We knew enough to look for a place where the soil was freshly turned. We found it."

Richie Sears gently sidled his horse closer, watching Crashaw. Sears' right arm was muffled to the elbow in a thick bandage, and he wore a sling around it. In the seamed mask of his face his eyes were ugly with pain. Soderstrom had made little detail of his fight with the gunman, and Crashaw thought, *So his gun arm was busted,* but this was a thin solace in a situation that was, he knew, as dangerous as any he had faced. He made his voice mild and purposeful:

"Loftus, it's clear enough. You're aiming to send your boys to take Soderstrom out of jail. Listen. If he's guilty, then—"

Old Buckmaster spoke for the first time, in a dead, exhausted voice. "Who'll stop me?"

"I will."

Buckmaster faintly jerked his head sideward, a gesture flecked with contempt. Crashaw slowly slipped his gun from its holster, cocking it deliberately. "I will," he repeated. "I'll stop you, even if every gun here is turned on me."

The old man's eyes squinted nearly shut under his brows. "What's your business, Crashaw? What d'you want here?"

Crashaw watched his face carefully. "You had your warning, Loftus. I told you I'm through taking sides."

"I know, I know. Get on with it." Under the heavy dullness of wrath, the old man's tone was irritated and puzzled.

"When a man kills a bunch of someone's cattle by pushing them off a canyon rim, he goes to jail. That plain enough?"

"It don't mean a goddamn thing, and I don't bluff a goddamn jot, Crashaw. Spell it out."

"Last night twenty to thirty head of Soderstrom's shorthorn beefs was pushed into Natchez Canyon. Your boy Chad led the party. Want to see the warrant?"

A slow, amazed anger flooded Chad Buckmaster's face. "That's a lie!"

"You were identified by Rafe Catron and old Waco."

"Then they're a pair of liars. Hell, I never stirred off the place last night, and I can prove it."

"You'll get that chance. Meantime you'll ride in with me." Crashaw paused, then said with a quiet irony, "Your pa observes the law, and the law says so."

"I will, like hell—"

"Steady down," Loftus declared heavily. "Crashaw, you're walking on Indian territory, and you better pull in your horns. No Buckmaster is going to spend one night in your fleabit lockup, so just pull in your horns."

There it was, the unequivocal challenge which, if Crashaw let it pass, would end forever any voice of authority he might have. "You pull in," he said flatly. "One thing you're not is a fool. Maybe there's more here than meets the eye. But Chad is coming with me."

Loftus gave Crashaw an unblinking, heavy-lidded stare intended to disconcert him. When it did not, he said with a massive impatience, "Don't be a damn fool, Otis. Come back into line, man. It can be the way it was all over."

"No," Crashaw said. "It'll never be that way again." And turned his gun on Chad as the younger Buckmaster's hand brushed back the skirt of his coat. "Don't," Crashaw said sharply, even as the dead-weary taste of hopelessness filled his mouth and his hand tensed for the moment when Chad's gun came up.

In that moment, his hot pained eyes glinting, Richie Sears whipped his left hand around to his right side and flipped up his gun with incredible speed. He fired twice.

For a fleeting instant Crashaw felt the hammerblows of

the bullets in his chest, and as he fell forward, heard Loftus roar belatedly, "Sears—no!" That sound was already fading, along with Naomi's scream and the dying light in his eyes, and it was all gone before his body hit the ground.

Fifteen

Soderstrom was pacing the narrow floor of his cell in a quiet rage when Thera's voice brought him to the barred window. He pulled up the sash. Hannah was there too, and he knew from the troubled anger in her face, and the shock close to tears in Thera's, that they had talked with Crashaw.

"Papa, we must help David if he—"

"I know, I know." Soderstrom ran a hand through his pale shaggy mane. "I must get out of here. You'll have to help me."

Thera bit her lip in dismay, for she had been reared to a strict respect for the law. "That is wrong, but . . . but there is David. You must find him, Papa. Maybe it's not too late."

Soderstrom glanced at Hannah, seeing no hesitancy at all. She said matter-of-factly, "There is probably a spare set of keys in Crashaw's desk. But his office door is locked."

Soderstrom growled under his breath, swinging restlessly away, then back again. "The lock of the outside door would not be hard to break, but how can you do it without attracting a lot of people?"

"It's still quite early for town folk," Hannah pointed out. "Haven't seen a soul on the street outside of us and Otis."

"It is too quiet this hour. The noise would bring somebody."

Thera's face brightened; she fumbled in the pale corona of her hair, and brought out a pin. With an intent care she pressed the tip against the jail wall, bending it back at an acute angle. Soderstrom scowled. "What are you doing there, girl?"

"I am going to open the front door with this little pin."

"Where the devil," Soderstrom began to roar, then caught himself. "Where did you learn such a trick, eh?"

She colored a little, but her eyes were very clear. "It's just something I picked up . . . oh, when I was small."

"Who taught you? Tell me that!"

"Uncle Haakon, Papa."

Soderstrom muttered, "Ahh—Haakon!" His wife's brother, a scamp and reprobate if ever there was one, dropping in from nowhere at odd times and departing just as suddenly. Well, it was no surprise. He glanced with brief embarrassment at Hannah, but she seemed only amused.

"I won't be but a moment," Thera promised, and hurried away. Hannah bent and lifted the white cloths that covered the two trays they had set on the ground. "Here . . . you must eat something." She began passing food through the bars, and Soderstrom ate quickly, washing it down with gulps of hot coffee.

Hannah smiled. "I like to see a man eat as though he means it. You flatter the cook, too."

"Thera. I know her cooking."

"Hm. I should be indignant, but if you can't tell which things which of us prepared, I guess that's a compliment."

"It's all good. So you cook?"

"Do you object to that, too?"

Soderstrom grinned, glancing over his shoulder as the office doorlatch made a gentle rattle. "A man can change his mind. Maybe it's good if a woman knows some things besides cooking and keeping house. I would be in a fix if my daughter had never learned to pick a lock."

Hannah laughed, and now he said soberly, "Nobody can say what may happen next. So now I will ask again, while there's time."

"I'd rather you didn't." She shook her head with a frowning indecision. "Yesterday you told me about sparing my father's men who raided your herd, when you had them at your mercy."

"I did not mean to use that on you," he said forcefully. "I was only telling what happened. Now are you asking why?"

"Yes."

"Then I'll tell you. Those men are alive because of what you said. That my actions would prove something."

"If that's true, I'm glad, But does it really mean a change? That would be a big one for you, and how can you be sure?"

"It was a change. I know, because I found it easy to do. If it was not a change, I would not be asking the question again."

"I wish you hadn't asked . . . so soon. I wish I could feel as sure as you do."

Again the latch rattled, and Thera swung the door gently inward, then stepped inside and quickly closed it. In a few seconds she found a spare ring of keys in the litter of a desk drawer. After an experimental minute or two the right key was fitted in the lock, and Soderstrom opened the cell door and went to the gunrack where Crashaw had placed his rifle. With the familiar assurance of the weapon against his palm, he moved to the office door to inspect the deserted street, then stepped outside with Thera. They slipped into the areaway between the jail and the adjacent building, where Hannah waited now. Soderstrom talked quickly.

"When I find McIver, I'll bring him to the ranch. It is a lot closer than the town to last night's bedground, and if he's hurt bad, those miles could make much difference. Go to the ranch and wait for us, Thera. Have everything ready to treat a gunshot wound."

"But what will you do then?" Hannah asked.

Soderstrom shrugged stolidly. "Give myself up. But no time to lose. Go back to your newspaper now."

"Can't I do something?"

"Yes. Stay in town and keep your eyes open." He hesitated. "If anything happens I should know, bring word to the ranch. Now, Thera, wait five minutes after I ride out, then get your horse."

Soderstrom expected no difficulty from the half-witted lad who was night hostler at the livery barn, and he got none. Smiling stupidly around his yawns, the boy saddled Soderstrom's horse. Soderstrom paid him and rode out at an easy pace, not lifting to a quick lope till he was beyond the last building.

Riding steadily northeast, he studied the metallic gloom that was thickening the sky, and thought glumly, *What a time for a storm.*

Inside of three miles, he saw a rider on the flats ahead, and knew it was Catron. He was not rushing himself, Soderstrom thought with a grim displeasure. He overtook Catron shortly. While explaining his escape, he did not miss a puzzling hint of sullenness behind the redheaded puncher's surprise.

As they rode on, Rafe glanced at the sky and shook his head. "If that's a bad one coming, we'll have a time finding him. He was hurt bad, or he should of controlled his horse when it bolted—least he would of found his way back. Of course we got to try, against any chance at all."

"The storm may hold off till tonight," Soderstrom said, knowing this was a thin hope.

Back at camp they found Waco Millard hunkered by the fire watching the coffee come to a boil. They squatted by the fire, and Waco asked why Soderstrom was out of jail, then remarked diffidently, "Well, I couldn't find nothing."

"So I see," Soderstrom said curtly. He poured some of the scalding brew and drank, letting it jar his thoughts to the need for organizing his next move. "Catron, you saw which way he was headed?"

"Directly west," Rafe said, and pointed. "We was about there when the raiders struck. Several of 'em engaged us while the others went after the herd. Of course it was dark and we was shooting blind, but Mac was hit right away. I left off the fight and went after him, but his horse was running hard, and I lost him. By the time I got back, the night riders was gone with them cattle."

Soderstrom was silent, studying the rugged dark lift of the badlands to the west. They would have their work cut out, trying to find a lone man in all that. Beyond lay the vast northern sweep of Wagontree graze, but it was unlikely that McIver had gotten that far.

He drank half his coffee and tossed the rest out and swung back to his horse. "Let's get to it."

Rafe said, "What about the shorthorns, Mr. Soderstrom? They'll get straying."

"Let them. Finding McIver comes first."

When they were in saddle, Soderstrom gave his orders. The three of them would separate and work out toward the west, each confining his search to a general area and covering it thoroughly. The man who found McIver would signal the others with two quick shots.

For hours Soderstrom drove himself with a relentless fury, pushing his horse through brush, over jagged abutments, down cramped and winding gorges. Where his horse could not go, he dismounted and reconnoitered on foot. When hunger pangs came, he dug out jerky and cold biscuits and ate without leaving his saddle.

Later, exhausted and discouraged, he rode back toward camp. He had explored to the edge of the west foothills where they shouldered against the peaks. A lone searcher could not cover every pocket of ground in a large area where a wounded man might lie up. Even his horse would not be easily spotted amid this rugged upheaval. Still, if alive, McIver could fire his rifle. If he were not dead, he must be close to it. Soderstrom's hopes had threaded fine.

And now the storm broke at last. The rain fell in blinding cascades, and a high wind lashed it against his slickered body. Soderstrom was half-drenched when he reached camp. The gear and provisions were gone, and the fire was a sodden heap of ashes.

Pulling up, he heard a voice hail him, and Rafe, his yellow slicker flapping formlessly in the wind, stepped from the nearby stand of trees. Waco was there too; they had toted the gear into the semi-shelter of the trees. Here, the force of rain and wind were broken, but the water seeped steadily down through the soaked branches, and the three men could only squat in unwarmed misery and wait it out. The sky writhed with white veins of lightning; thunder cannonaded deafeningly, and softened to a sullen mutter as the storm's first fury ebbed. The wind died off and the rain rattled on the leaves and sobbed on the drenched ground.

Rafe ended the long silence, and his tone was surly: "Well?"

"I don't know." Soderstrom rubbed a hand over his wet face, a gray and hopeless conviction in him.

Rafe said, "We looked all over, and not a sign. Anyhow a man can't track in this miserable rain, even if the sign wasn't wiped out."

"That sure shines to me," Waco shrilled softly. "I hanker for some hot grub and a warm blanket."

Soderstrom eyed the pair of them narrowly, positive without knowing why that they were concealing something behind this sullen, uneasy reluctance to pursue the search. Still, there was some meat to their argument. It looked increasingly hopeless, and this was not a thing to which a man should be forced against his will.

For himself, he would not quit until McIver was found, dead or alive. He said so, adding curtly, "When the storm stops, you two will get the herd on to Ladder. The north range is only a few miles. Scatter it there, then do what you like." At this moment, he did not give a particular damn what either man did.

Shortly the rain thinned to a faint drizzle. A smoky mist curled off the ground as the men rose from their cramped squat, wet and chilled to the bone. Soderstrom and Waco rubbed down the steaming, shivering horses, while Rafe found a rotted deadfall and kicked it apart. It yielded enough tinder-dry wood for a fire, and they had kept their food, gear and spare clothes dry by rolling them in their ground tarps.

With dry clothes on their backs and warm food in their bellies, they separated, Rafe and Waco moving the herd out while Soderstrom prepared to take up the hunt still farther west. There was the possibility, however slight, that McIver had stayed on his horse while it strayed that far.

Soderstrom buttoned his jumper to his neck against a raw rising wind, then followed a canyon trail west. The clouds were shredding before the brisk wind, turning the sky a neutral gray. He swung north and south in slow zigzags, occasionally firing off his pistol.

This time, when he returned to the deserted camp, his discouragement was total. He sank down on his haunches, rubbing his bent head between his hands. Maybe it was only the miserable weather coupled with his crowding weariness, but for the first time he felt his iron control slipping, a feel of defeated misery seeping through him. He was fed up with burned-out hopes, tired of fighting, sick of his own part in a deadlocked conflict. What would it mean, getting the short-horns through safely, if he had to return to the ranch without McIver and face his daughter's eyes? And it was this, the thought of Thera, that drove him back to his feet. There were still a few hours of daylight, and he would use them. He would pack up the remaining provisions and comb over a limited area, stopping wherever the need for meals or sleep dictated.

Making up a sack of grub, he tied it on his saddle and rode out of the cottonwoods. He had gone a short way when he saw the plodding horse coming up from the northwest. The rider was slumped across the pommel, and seeing only this much, Soderstrom savagely roweled his animal around and headed back.

McIver's head was bowed against his chest, and he lifted it with a drowsy effort. His face was almost colorless, but the ghost of a grin flickered there. "Still a hell of an adventure, Mr. Soderstrom . . . working for you."

Sixteen

After the rain wetted down the deep dust of Mimbreno's street, hooves, boots, and wheels chopped it to a chocolate mire. Hannah, carrying a sack of groceries, picked her way over the oozing islands between glassy-puddled ruts, and paused on the opposite walk to scrape the mud off her shoes. "Uncle Bill" Goodrich, standing in the doorway of his store, said good-naturedly, "You're too old for puddle-hopping, Hannah. Where are all the young Raleighs in this town?"

Hannah made a wry face. "Lord knows. Isn't there a cloak or two in your stock, Uncle Bill?"

The old man chuckled. "And I'm too old to do myself any good by getting chivalrous, worse luck." His glance passed down the street where a body of riders was swinging into town. He said briefly, "Your clan, looks like," and spat carefully in the street, then wheeled ponderously into his store.

There were an even dozen of them, and Chad was heading them. Riding close to his stirrup was Richie Sears, his arm heavily bandaged. Her brother did not look at her as they rode past. All of these men were new hands, except three who lagged somewhat behind the others, as if ashamed.

Impulsively Hannah hailed one of them, a man who had punched Wagontree cattle when she was a child. She felt a vague reluctance in his manner as he reined over to the sidewalk. She said bluntly, "Red, what is this? And where's Otis Crashaw? I know he went out to Wagontree."

"Yes, ma'am. You can see for yourself what we're about." Red motioned with a horny hand, and she saw that the Wagontree men had halted by the sheriff's office. Chad dropped off his mount, tossing his reins to a crewman, and tramped into the building.

Hannah felt a coldness of premonition. "Red. What about Otis? What happened?"

"Dead, Miss Hannah." Red rubbed a finger vaguely along the rusty droop of his mustache, and shook his head. "That Sears. Crashaw, he wanted to take Chad in for stampedin' some of this Swedish fella's cattle off a cliff, he said, and Chad said he hadn't done it. Then Sears pulled on Crashaw. He was a tough old dog, but he didn't have no chance."

Hannah said slowly, "No," feeling a qualm of sickness. "But I still don't see what you're doing here—"

At that moment Chad emerged from the jail; he rapped orders at the men, who dismounted. They began fanning out in pairs and threes, heading for different buildings.

"Your brother's been found, Miss Hannah," Red said, watching the others. "Now don't tell me that Swedish fella has got away."

"Garth found? Found . . . how?"

"Shot to death, ma'am. I don't know. This don't seem like the way to handle it, but your pa is plenty upset."

Hannah simply watched him in stunned silence, and he went on lamely, "Well, he sent us to fetch Soderstrom out to Wagontree."

Hannah found her voice. "For what?"

"Now you know your pappy better than to ask, Miss Hannah." Red seemed embarrassed, and touching his hat, he rode on to the jail.

For a few blank moments Hannah stood watching the Wagontree men disperse into the buildings, searching for the missing prisoner, and then she turned slowly into the newspaper office. She set her groceries on the littered desk, knowing with a deep-reaching fear that the finding of Garth's body meant that no Wagontree men would be permitted to rest until Soderstrom was dead or captured.

Hannah kneaded her knuckles against her palms. She had to do something. Soderstrom would take his wounded man to Ladder if he found him, and he had said to bring any word there. He had to be warned—if only she could find him before any Wagontree man did. With that thought, she was tearing off her paper cuffs and ink-soiled apron. She started toward her quarters at the rear, but somebody's quick, urgent rapping on the office door brought her impatiently hurrying back to open it.

Naomi stood there in her riding habit, hatless, and seeing the bright cold terror in her face, Hannah let her first words die unsaid. She beckoned her inside, and closed the door behind her. "Naomi, good Lord. What is it?"

"Oh God," her sister-in-law moaned. "I wish I were dead. First Garth, then Crashaw, now Soder—oh my God, Han! I want to die!"

Angrily, Hannah caught her by the shoulders and shook her. "What *is* the matter with you? Control yourself!" Naomi only wailed.

Hannah thought, *All right then,* and slapped her, hard. Naomi stepped back, blinking in shock; her mouth fell open.

"There's been enough dying," Hannah said matter-of-factly.

"Soderstrom is out of jail. He's still alive—for a while at least."

"Oh, thank God for that!"

"Hurry now, tell me what this is all about."

Within a few minutes she knew all that could be gotten out of Naomi, and she said bitterly, "You knew the truth? You even saw it happen—and you didn't say a word? Do you realize—"

"Yes, yes! But I didn't before, Han. I swear! All that Chad told me was not to worry, he'd arrange things so that nobody could ever find out how Garth had met his death. He didn't tell me he was going to fix the blame on Soderstrom. I didn't know what he'd really done until he brought in Garth's body and told your father about finding him by Soderstrom's place."

"I can believe that. You're foolish enough to be bamboozled in exactly that way." Hannah's tone was hard and accusing; for once her easy, charitable nature could find no pity for this girl whose acquiescence and weakness had finally pulled others besides herself into deep trouble. "But once you knew what Chad had done, you could have told my father. I needn't ask—I know you couldn't find the courage."

Naomi walked aimlessly back and forth, sobbing like a small girl. "I c-couldn't, Han, I'm a-f-fraid of h-h-him."

"Of who?" Hannah demanded acidly. "Chad or Pa?"

The door opened quietly, and Hannah turned her head. Chad stood in the doorway with his scuffed muddy boots planted apart, and his bulk seemed to fill the room. His eyes were abnormally bright, and there was a hint of wicked violence in his thin smile. "Hello, girls."

"Hello, goodbye," Hannah snapped, hiding the cold alarm she felt.

"Don't get pleasant, sister. Soderstrom around here?"

"Why should he be?"

"He's not in the jail, for one thing." Chad moved idly past them into the room and paused, hands on hips, eyeing the typestand thoughtfully. "For another, you kind of shine to that big Swenska, don't you? I just wondered."

Hannah said with a forced mockery, "Why, do you believe all you hear?"

Chad continued to stare curiously at the typestand, letting one shoulder lift and settle lazily. "I dunno. Point is, if he didn't make tracks out of town, he's hid out somewhere around here. What do you think?"

"I really couldn't say."

"Uh huh." Chad sauntered back to the doorway that opened on Hannah's quarters and looked inside. Watching him, she had the uneasy realization that Chad would only have had to question the night hostler at the stable to know that Soderstrom had gotten a horse and ridden out. If he knew that, then he had come here because he had seen Naomi enter the office, and was wondering whether she had come to Hannah, her friend, to relieve her burdened conscience. He might even have caught a little of what they'd been saying.

Chad came back to the typestand and leaned his shoulder against it, folding his arms. "Well, you can't always go by what folks say." He gave Naomi a negligent glance. Her face was bloodless; she was, Hannah saw, actually petrified with fear. "What's the matter with her?"

"She doesn't see her husband's dead body brought in every day of the week," Hannah said coldly. "It's also quite an occasion in a girl's life when the sheriff gets killed trying to arrest her brother-in-law."

"That could be," Chad said agreeably, then gave a powerful heave of his shoulder. The typestand tilted and then crashed over on the stone composing table, the upper and lower case trays banging down and littering the floor with hundreds of pieces of type.

Hannah could only stare in stunned, appalled silence as he strolled over to her desk then, remarking, "On the other hand, we know how our sister-in-law here is kind of prone to imagine things, if you can guess what I mean." He picked up the desk chair and smashed it down on the desk. A rung and a leg broke. "And when she gets imagining, she gets to running off at the mouth, too." He clubbed the chair down three times more, splintering it to kindling. He picked up the only other chair and swung it against the wooden railing. "I sure don't believe all I hear, and I hope you don't, Han. Furniture's cheap, if you can guess what I mean. A body's life, now, that's another case." He proceeded to carefully smash the chair and railing to fragments.

The spell that held Naomi broke, and she ran forward, crying, "No, Chad—"

He did not even look at her as he swung his arm sideways, his hand still closed around a heavy piece of the chair. His fist caught her backhanded across the mouth. She screamed and fell, and lay face down moaning in the litter of metal slugs.

Hannah looked on helplessly, in shocked disbelief, as Chad went about systematically wrecking the office. He could do little damage to the heavy press, but he broke the filled forms to pieces on it, types and quadrats flying everywhere. He finished up by dumping all the paper stock on the floor, pouring ink over it, and stamping it to a black soggy pulp. He did all this with a child's destructive pleasure contained by a man's cold ferocity.

Afterward he walked over to Naomi. She still lay where she had fallen, motionless with terror, and he prodded her with his toe. "You want to be careful what you go telling people after this, honey. Otherwise I'll just naturally have to do something drastic."

He looked slowly at Hannah now, and something chill and repellent was in his eyes. She had not been really afraid until this moment. He raised his arm, pointing his finger at her like a gun. "You mind what I tell you. Don't say a word. Don't print a word. Your life wouldn't be worth it." He went out the door, closing it softly behind him.

Why, Hannah thought with a peculiar detachment, *why he is crazy.* The dark coldness of the conviction felt strange in the harsh gray reality of this midday. Only a madman could pledge raw murder in a tone of calm indifference and still leave you unshakably convinced of his sincerity. Pure desperation, she supposed, could do that to someone.

Recovering, she went to Naomi and helped her to her feet and into the living quarters. Hannah settled her on a chair and got a cold wet towel. Naomi held it to her split, bleeding lip, whimpering softly, eyes still blank with shock.

It made little difference whether something he'd overheard or only a brooding suspicion had led Chad to this open, brutal act of intimidation, Hannah thought bleakly. If he dared to do this much, in town and in broad daylight, there was an excellent chance that he'd try to silence for good the one witness to his brother's killing, and at the first opportunity. Not only Naomi, but herself as well, now.

She drew up a chair in front of Naomi and sat so the other girl had to face her. "Listen to me. You must go to Pa and tell him the truth."

Naomi roused with a jerk, and her eyes seemed to withdraw into a recess of fear. "I can't . . . Han. I'm more afraid of him than of Chad."

"He'd do nothing to you," Hannah said with asperity. "That's part of his code; treat a woman like a stick of household furniture, but never abuse her physically. Anyway, your only wrong was in covering up for Chad. You've got to make it right now, or Pa won't stop till Krag Soderstrom is dead. If he knows the truth, he'll call off his men. Are your tender fears worth a man's life?" And quietly, pointedly, she added, "Don't delude yourself any further about Chad, or what he's capable of. Don't forget, you're the only witness to the killing."

Naomi burst out, "But it was self-defense, Han! I'd testify that Chad had to shoot. I don't see why he . . ."

"He framed Soderstrom for the killing, and he'd draw a prison term for that. But even that's a small part of his thinking. Pa would disinherit him if he knew the truth, and especially how the situation came about, if he didn't shoot him like a dog. I know my dear father."

Still doubtfully, Naomi murmured, "But Chad wouldn't . . ."

"He would," Hannah snapped. "If you doubt that after what you just saw, you're an idiot. Neither of our lives will be safe as long as you keep Chad's secret. Can't you get that through your head?"

Naomi was still plainly afraid, but Hannah knew she was scoring; and with only a little more persuasion, was able to secure Naomi's reluctant agreement. The two of them went up front to the office, and peering out the window, Hannah saw that Chad, a short distance down the street, had gathered the Wagontree men around him, issuing orders.

"Go out and get on your horse," she told Naomi, "and ride out past them slowly. If you're asked, you're going home, that's all. Chad thinks he's thrown the fear of God into you. See that you look like it." She added dryly, "You shouldn't have a lot of trouble there."

"What will you do, Han?"

"Soderstrom couldn't know that the Wagontree crew is looking for him; he has to be warned. He'll probably be bringing a wounded crewman of his to Ladder, so I'll go there. At least his daughter will be there, and—but never mind. Get going now."

Hannah watched, holding her breath, as Naomi mounted and rode slowly toward the end of town. Chad gave her a fleeting glance as she passed, then ignored her. Nobody spoke to her, and in a minute she was out of sight.

Hannah released her breath, but caught it again with her realization that Soderstrom's ranch would be one of the first places to which Chad would dispatch searchers, and she had no time to lose.

She hurried back through the building and let herself out the rear door; there was no time to change to her riding costume. She swiftly skirted the rear of the buildings till she reached the livery barn, entering it through the runway entrance at the back.

The day hostler, three-quarters drunk and blinking owlishly, was forking hay into a stall. He grinned, "Hallo there, Miss Han."

"I want a horse, Lex. No, no sidesaddle. Give me a man's."

Lex gave her a long look of rheumy disapproval as he moved to the saddle pole. Hannah fretted with impatience as he laboriously saddled a jughead paint. She snatched the reins from him and bunched her skirts in one hand, drawing a deep breath as she toed into stirrup and swung awkwardly up.

"Miss Hannah, that's—"

"Oh, shut up!"

Hannah reined along a few gingerly paces till she had her seat, then swung out through the back archway. She rode slowly till she was past the last of the houses, then urged the paint onto a road fetlock-deep in mud, gratful only that she wasn't contending with a sidesaddle while trying to get a little speed. The man who had decided that women had limbs and not legs was merely a fool; the one who thought up the sidesaddle had a streak of downright cruelty, she thought, trying furiously to straighten her wadded skirt and petticoats.

Then she realized, with a sinking fear, that she could not have chosen a poorer mount for the purpose. No matter how she drummed his flanks or talked to him, the jughead could be stirred barely beyond his stolid, plodding pace. It was too late to undo the mistake, and she could only hold to a dwindling hope that Soderstrom would for some reason not come to his ranch. Something like a sob broke in her throat, and she hated to think why.

A faint rain was still falling, wetting her slowly. She shivered miserably, wondering what her father would do if he ran down and killed Soderstrom. Probably buy enough alibis and lying witnesses to cover himself; he might even make it appear that it was Soderstrom, not Chad, whom Otis Crashaw had gone to arrest, and that Soderstrom, not Sears, had killed the sheriff. In that event, he could make the claim that Soderstrom had later resisted citizen's arrest by her father's men, and they had been forced to shoot. *Yes,* Hannah thought dully, *he would think of something like that.*

Perhaps five minutes later, as she had expected, a half-dozen riders came into sight on the muddy switchbacks behind her. Shortly, without speaking, the body of men had ranged their mounts up beside and around her, quietly but effectively surrounding her. Resignedly, Hannah brought the sluggish jughead to a halt.

Richie Sears appeared to be in charge. He touched his hat and said with soft courtesy, "What you doing out here, ma'am?"

"Enjoying the weather," Hannah said in a wintry voice. "Where is Little Chadwick?"

"He cut out for north of here, in case the Swede headed for his last trail camp. He sent me to Ladder, seeing that our man might go there, too." Sears' temper, no longer masked by his dead cynicism, lay plain and wicked in his pain-drawn face and murky eyes. "Chad knows I would fancy doing a job on that snork, even if your pa wants him alive. Well, ma'am, seeing as you're heading our way, we'll just give you some company."

Seventeen

When Soderstrom had spread a fairly dry pack tarp on the ground and eased McIver onto it, he found that the bullet had passed clean through, low on the left side. He said quietly, "It could be worse, boy. Thera can tend you good as any saw-bones. I'll do what I can now."

McIver's face was slick and sickly in the gray wet light, and his teeth were set against the pain. "Maybe you should raise my pay," he said faintly, "for getting shot at."

Soderstrom remembered, with a sudden mixture of feelings, that McIver was still working for nothing but his food and a bunk. "Anytime you don't like it, you can quit," he growled.

McIver smiled around his pain. Soderstrom applied a bandage of sorts. "Now rest a while, and we'll be going home. Maybe you can sleep a little, eh?"

But McIver, despite a distant and drowsy look now, was not ready for sleep. He wanted to talk, and he had enough left to tell what he knew, though he was rambling almost incoherently toward the end. After eluding Rafe and Waco last night, he had simply staggered and crawled through a forest of rock until his wound had sapped his strength completely. Afterward he had been unconscious or delirious for hours, finally coming to his senses to find his horse nuzzling him where he'd fallen. He had not fired his rifle, for fear the shots would bring Rafe or Waco. After a dozen tries, he had made it into the saddle and given the animal its head. He remembered little more until the horse had plodded into the old camp and Soderstrom had found him.

Soderstrom, not an easily affected man, felt a little sick. He had not considered that Catron's and Millard's hatred for Buckmaster might carry them this far. Lord knew what would come of it.

He let McIver have an hour's sleep under the misting sky, then reluctantly aroused him. The boy had gotten some sleep, but his eyes were glazed, his breathing labored, as Soderstrom dragged him upright. He muttered, "Don't think I'll make it, sir."

"Good," Soderstrom said. "It will be good to have Thera learn what a yellowbelly you are."

McIver's eyes seemed to burn away the fever; but as if he saw behind Soderstrom's words, he made a show of vitality then, his whole body tensed against the pain as Soderstrom gave him a lift into the saddle.

They rode south at an inching pace, McIver rocking loosely in the saddle to minimize the pain, Soderstrom making aimless talk to divert him. But McIver was dully silent, his chin sagging on his chest. Soderstrom watched him with a deepening worry, and he was ready when the boy began to cant sideways in his saddle.

He reined over and halted McIver's horse and spoke sharply. No answer, and Soderstrom dismounted and worked swiftly, tying the boy's feet together beneath his horse's barrel, then lashing his wrists to the saddle horn. It was crude and unpleasant, but it would have to do. The bandage was bloody, which could not be helped, either.

Again in the saddle, leading McIver's horse, he rode on. The rain had ceased entirely, but weariness added to the aches of his body, fast dulling his senses.

He snapped alert, realizing that he was dozing off. He had passed through a skimpy motte of mostly dead trees, with a rank undergrowth of heavy brush, and in this moment as he reached the end of the motte, he picked up the bunch of slickered riders heading north through the misty drizzle, swinging past the motte at perhaps fifty yards' distance.

Instinctively Soderstrom pulled back into the brush, watching them till they were lost in the mizzling veil of rain. Then he rode on, his eyes and thoughts totally alert. He could not have told exactly why he had avoided contact with those men ... but why in this lonely country and miserable weather was a sizable group of horsemen heading north, away from any settlement, and in the direction from which he had just come?

An interminable time passed, it seemed to Soderstrom, before he achieved the rim of drab low hills behind Ladder headquarters. The dampness was deep in his bones now, numbing them, so that he felt only a meaningless drift of sensations. He was barely hanging onto wakefulness as he crossed the hills, and then by a wrenching effort, dragged himself alert once more.

Thinking of the riders he had seen made him wary; he swung in a watchful half-circle of the place before approaching it finally. He was still careful then, holding off a ways as he rode along back of the outsheds and corrals, sizing them up. If there were men here, there would be horses too. There was no sign of either. The buildings lay solid and still in the moist twilight, and the windows of the house shed cheery squares of light. So Thera was there, waiting his arrival.

McIver startled him by saying suddenly, weakly, "We're home?"

"Yes, home." The boy's strong rally was a heartening thing, Soderstrom thought as he dismounted by the corral. He opened the gate and led both animals inside. Rafe's and Waco's saddle mounts, along with the two pack horses, were here, he noticed; they had arrived all right, and the clinging tension washed out of him.

His own rawboned roan, which had carried a brutal load of work for many days, was on its last legs. After he had gotten McIver into the house he would see to proper care for both mounts. Now he could spare the time to remove the galling saddles. He uncinched and swung off his own hull, and was coming around on his heel when a voice saluted him softly.

"Hello, snork."

Soderstrom carefully finished his turn. Richie Sears leaned in the doorway of the stable only yards away, his gun loosely trained in his left hand. "Arm hurts to beat hell, snork. Will for a long time. Now," he brought the gun up steadily, "where do you reckon a man will die slowest from a bullet?"

Soderstrom said, "Think you can handle this all by yourself?"

Sears' chuckle was a thin and whispery sound. "There's others. You was covered from the time you rode off them hills. Others is laid up around the place where I told 'em to. Horses are hid, too. That's just insurance. I want you all to myself, snork, so I stationed myself where there wouldn't be no question of it. Old Man Buckmaster wants you brought to him alive, but I don't see letting him have the pleasure."

Soderstrom had supposed that this was Sears' personal vendetta, his alone, and he said in puzzlement, "Buckmaster? Why? He gave Crashaw his word—"

"Garth's been found. Up on that ridge yonder. Shot dead. You wasn't fooling, was you snork?"

Soderstrom felt clammy sweat form between his palms and the smooth saddle. "The sheriff will still not like this, Sears."

Sears' laugh made his spine crawl. "He won't mind. He took sick all at once out at Wagontree. It was fatal as hell."

"You, Sears?"

Sears laughed again.

"So, you mean to cheat your boss of his pleasure. You better have a good story, then."

"I got one already." Sears' cartwheel spurs jingled softly as he walked forward. He halted a couple of yards away. "Nobody can see us from here, and I give the others an order not to close in till I call 'em. Said no sense in being messy if one man could take you prisoner. My story, you made a break just as I sung out to bring 'em. Understand? I had to kill you."

He thumbed the hammer to full cock, then half-turned his head to summon his men. And Soderstrom, with nothing to lose now, made his move. The saddle was hugged chest-high to his body, and he flung it out with the heels of his hands and

146

took a long step sideways. A strained grunt left Sears as the heavy rig hit his body and arm, bearing down his gun so that the bullet exploded into the mud.

Soderstrom made a swift long lunge; his fist meeting Sears' neck in a savage chop. The gunman went down, and Soderstrom wheeled for McIver's horse, snatching up the reins. He could hear running steps across the yard, and there was no time to lose. He yanked his rifle from its scabbard, then pulled McIver's horse along with him into the stable, hauling the door shut after him. He stood in the dim runway and listened, his rifle ready. From outside came a flurry of excited voices as his men found Sears. Quite abruptly the voices broke apart as the men scattered off.

They had a fair certainty of where he was, Soderstrom grimly guessed, but none were foolhardy enough to make a head-on entry into the stable. In a very few moments, things would get too hot for comfort. Working swifly, he untied McIver from the saddle and carried him into the deep shelter of a stall. "Give me a gun," the youth whispered as Soderstrom lowered him onto a heap of straw.

"No. You stay here and keep yourself down." Straightening then, Soderstrom froze as a rasp of strained breathing reached him in the dim musty stillness.

Somebody else was in the stable, and Soderstrom catfooted swiftly to where he had left his rifle. Training it on a dark corner, he said softly, "All right, whoever that is. Come out now."

"Don't know as I can make it that far, Mr. Soderstrom," Rafe Catron husked weakly. In a moment Soderstrom was kneeling in the corner, striking a match. He found Rafe tied hand and foot on the floor, his shirt caked with dried blood. Beside him, wide-eyed and sightless in the grotesque sprawl of death, was the body of Waco Millard. He had been shot through the head.

As Soderstrom pulled out his claspknife and freed Rafe, the redhead whispered, "We scattered the cattle like you ordered and come directly on to the place. They was laid up waiting. When that guntipper Sears ordered us to stand fast, we made a break instead. They dropped me off my horse and done for poor old Waco."

"No talk now. Can you handle a gun?"

"Give me a hand over to that front wall. There's a few choice knotholes there."

Soderstrom assisted him over to the wall and fetched McIver's rifle from the scabbard on his horse. It struck him that things were too quiet out in the yard, and he put his eye to a knothole. A man was coming stealthily toward the building at a half-crouching trot. Soderstrom nudged his rifle muzzle to the knothole and fired above the man's head, and watched his wild retreat.

This must have been only a hopeful maneuver to take him by surprise, for now that it had failed, they opened up a concerted fire at the thin stable walls. Soderstrom and Catron hugged the dirt floor while the rain of slugs through the wall above showered their prone bodies with rotted splinters.

Almost as suddenly, the shooting slacked off. Soderstrom eased onto his haunches and peered out the knothole, as a body of riders thundered into the yard. He heard one of the newcomers shout a question, and recognized the voice as Chad Buckmaster's. It came to him that the Wagontree force must have been split, with Sears heading up the group dispatched to Ladder, while the others, led by Chad, had headed for his recent trail camp. That would be the bunch that had passed him earlier and now, finding nothing, had come to join Sears' men at Wagontree. If there was one thing they had not needed, Soderstrom thought dourly, it was reinforcements.

Now there was a long respite in the shooting, apparently ordered by Chad so he could size things up. Soderstrom sank down against the wall, a gray hopelessness in him. Loftus Buckmaster wanted his blood, and with all pretense of law in Buckmaster County wiped out by Crashaw's death, what could stop him? What chance did Soderstrom and two wounded men stand against Buckmaster's whole crew? This lawless vacuum was a temporary thing: the U.S. marshal, and probably the Army, would step in before long—but too late to do Krag Soderstrom any good. He could only wait in the hot breathing gloom of the stable, wait for a fighting death.

Soderstrom was a fatalist, therefore not a praying man. Still he came close to praying that, whatever happened now, Thera would not come to harm. He felt a weary sadness that he had never found the right words with Hannah, but then that had been his trouble in most things, and his own fault. He had always prized actions, not words. *So much to say, and now there is no time.*

He was, he realized, afraid as he had been only twice before in his life. Once when Hedda had lain dying, and he could do nothing. And again during those twenty agonizing seconds when he had believed that his daughter's body lay crushed beneath tons of dynamited rock. Now, for the first time, he was afraid for himself. And he thought of the old Vikings, the berserkers who in the lust of battle, shouting above their shields, would "run to meet their fates." *They were something, those old boys,* he thought; a smile straightened his lips at the thought of his kinship with those mad fighters, and the fear ran out of him.

He became aware that Rafe Catron, weakened by loss of blood, was speaking faintly. ". . . Better tell you while there's time. Don't fancy going out with it on my soul."

"I know," Soderstrom said stonily. "Don't waste your breath."

"Mac told you, huh? Jesus, I was sorry about that. We looked for him come daylight, before I rode in to tell the sheriff. Not finding him, I concluded he had laid up in cover somewheres and died there. So I carried through the plan." Rafe sighed. "Poor crazy old Waco. He shot Mac, you know, but I don't blame him none. It was my idea, so really my doing. Couldn't stop myself."

"What about Crashaw? You couldn't help that, either, eh?"

"Crashaw?"

"He went to arrest Chad Buckmaster on your lie, that you already know. Sears killed him. No—I think you and Waco done that."

"Lord God," Rafe whispered.

Soderstrom thought, *There is one thing I can do,* and raised himself to his knees, placing his mouth to the knothole. "Buckmaster! Chad Buckmaster!"

"Want to give up, Swede?"

"No. But listen. There are two wounded men with me, Catron and McIver. Let them be taken out before—"

A fusillade of blistering fire cut short his words. Again Soderstrom flattened along the dank floor as slugs hammered the old walls. He moved along the knotholed wall, firing at the gunflashes, then shifting along quickly before they had his position. He saw a dim form sprint across the yard in the slow dusk; he hesitated, but this was war. He sighted carefully in the bad light, then pulled the trigger. The man stumbled and went down, then started crawling back to cover, dragging a broken leg.

The shooting was too heavy, and Soderstrom dived back to the floor. Next, he thought, his sweating face against the dirt, somebody would think of firing the stable, and it would be all up. This was no good. *Give up, then. Maybe these two will be saved anyway—maybe they will not kill two wounded men in cold blood. Give up now.*

He was about to get his feet under him to call out, when, dimly above the shots, he heard a deep voice roaring an order. All at once the shooting died, and Soderstrom came to his knees and set his eye to the hole. He saw that a buckboard with two people had pulled into the yard, coming to a stop squarely between the Wagontree men and the stable.

"What's happening?" Rafe murmured.

"I don't know. But old Loftus himself has come. Now we'll see. . . ."

A faint creak of rusty hinged metal warned Soderstrom. He came pivoting around on his haunches. Someone had stealthily pushed open the door. It was easy to identify the whip-lean silhouette in the doorway as Richie Sears. The gunman's vision must have been momentarily baffled by the gloom, but the gritty sound of Soderstrom's heels as he turned gave a target. Gunflame erupted from the level of Sears' hip. The bullet hammered into the wall close by Soderstrom's head, and frantically he levered his rifle.

A shot roared almost in his ear. Rafe was on his knees, rifle in hands, his dim shape half bent in an agony of effort, as he shot once, twice, and then again, with a clean and deliberate care. Sears fired twice at Rafe's gunflashes, and then he

150

swayed and shuddered. His last shot angled into the floor, and he caught at the doorframe as he plunged downward. His hand slipped, and he pitched down on his face. His outflung hand twitched in the fading light, and was motionless.

Soderstrom gathered his shaky legs under him and rose, walking over to Sears. A reek of powdersmoke filled the stable. He bent briefly, and straightened. "You got him good, Catron. You—"

He paused, catching an odd, broken note in Catron's breathing. By the time Soderstrom reached him, he had toppled over on his side. Swiftly Soderstrom struck a match and held it low where Rafe's denim jacket fell open from his shirt. Both of Sears' bullets had found the mark. Even as he saw this, the last of Rafe's breath sighed away.

Eighteen

Soderstrom groped to the doorway and stood there, cupping his hands to his mouth. "Buckmaster! You hear me? I want to give up. I'll throw out my gun. I ask only that you not hurt this boy with me. He's hurt bad enough."

There was momentary silence before Loftus Buckmaster rumbled back, "I hear you, Swenska. You can come out any time. Throw your gun away or keep it, makes no difference. Been all the shooting there's going to be. What was that racket in there just now?"

Surprise held Soderstrom mute for a moment, and then he called, "Rafe Catron. And your man Sears. They have killed each other, mister."

"That's a fair exchange," said old Loftus. "All right, come along out. Need any help with that wounded what's-his-name?"

"McIver. I'll carry him out."

Gently Soderstrom lifted the feverish boy and carried him from the stable to the house. He stepped into the lamplit parlor and halted, taking in the room with a glance. Thera was seated on the leather sofa, and seeing Hannah beside her, he felt a wash of surprise. A Wagontree tough was also present in the room, evidently stationed to watch the girls. Both of them had a pale and shaken look, but were well enough otherwise, he saw with an intense relief.

Thera came to her feet with a soft cry, and he sternly told her, as he carried McIver into his own room, that this was no time for nonsense. Thera steadied at once; she had the proper dressings laid out and ready by the bed, and she said quietly, "Keep those people out of here, Papa," and went to work.

Soderstrom returned to the parlor. Several more toughs had entered the room, and they all eyed him guardedly. "You wait here, mister," one of them said curtly, and Soderstrom, bone-weary again, slacked onto the vacated sofa. Hannah had left the house, and now from the yard he heard old Buckmaster say, "Lend me your shoulder, sister, will you? Chadwick, I want to see you inside. Naomi, too. The rest of you stay out here."

There were heavy slow steps on the porch. Loftus entered, his arm around Hannah's shoulders, and with considerable difficulty she supported him across the room to a battered armchair. Naomi Buckmaster followed them closely, a white, pinched expression on her face. Chad stepped inside, too, looking angry and baffled. The old man planted his cane firmly, trembling a little as he eased his great weight into the chair. Drops of sweat glistened on his furrowed face; he shut his pain-dulled eyes for a few seconds. When they opened again, they were as bright and sharp as a hawk's.

"Red," he said quietly.

A staid-faced puncher, older than the others, drawled, "Boss?"

"Give me your gun."

Soderstrom's muscles grew tense, his hands tightening around the rifle across his knees. One of the toughs murmured, "Mister, don't move about like that."

"Shut up, Macklin," old Loftus said flatly. "Red, I want your gun."

The middle-aged puncher palmed it out of his belt and, crossing the room, slipped it into Loftus' outheld hand. The old man painfully adjusted his thick, arthritic fingers around the grip and, slowly, thumbed back the hammer. He swung the muzzle till it was fixed squarely on the broad chest of his son.

"Now, Chadwick. I trust you now. You bat a winker and I'll blow you apart where you stand."

The color drained from Chad's wide face. He faintly lifted and settled one shoulder. "Pa, I hate to spoil a good joke, but ain't you putting a gun on the wrong man?"

"I wish to hell I was. Now, Red, you take his gun. Mind you don't get between us, and go slow about it."

Red stepped carefully behind Chad and lifted his pistol from its holster. Old Loftus flicked a flinty glance at his daughter-in-law. "Now, you say in front of these witnesses just what you told me. Don't leave out a word, you hear?"

Naomi's glance slid to Chad, and her eyes held a stark fright, Soderstrom saw. She started to talk, her voice low and thin. Loftus broke in growling, "Now, damn it, girl, you speak out so everyone can hear. Talk up!"

And one by one, as Naomi spoke, the gazes in the room turned on Chad Buckmaster. But Soderstrom watched the face of old Loftus and his hand that was rock-steady now, and he thought, *When she has finished, the old man will kill him.*

Chad's eyes were hot and brilliant; his fleshily handsome face told nothing. Suddenly he laughed with a shattering mockery, throwing back his head and letting the laughter spill from him.

All he intended was to throw everyone off guard; this was clear an instant later when he wheeled with a spring-muscled grace for the doorway two feet away. He plunged out the door as the gun in Loftus' fist roared, the bullet chewing splinters from the door casing.

As swiftly as Chad had moved, Soderstrom was on his feet diving across the room and out the door. As his heel touched the porch, he veered in a quarter-turn, in time for a glimpse of Chad's bulky form vanishing around the house.

Soderstrom vaulted across the porch and off it, skirting around the corner in pursuit. The dusk had deepened almost to full dark, and he hauled up, briefly losing Chad in the shadows. Then he caught the thud of running feet and followed the sound. All of it had happened so quickly that the men lounging back in the yard only now broke a stunned quiet in an aimless chorus of curses and questions.

Soderstrom did not pause again. He knew from Chad's line of flight that he was heading for a stand of cottonwood a short distance upcreek. A moment later he caught a wild crashing of brush as Chad flailed his way along the thicket-choked bank. Soderstrom plunged after him, and soon saw the dark ragged silhouette of the grove ahead.

He had nearly reached the trees when a horse's whinny lifted out of the darkness, then Chad's savage curse. A moment later came the crackling passage of a heavy body through the trees. Soderstrom hauled up with the thought that when Sears, in laying his trap earlier, had had his men hide their mounts, at least one man had concealed his horse in this grove, where Chad had stumbled on it.

Soderstrom gave a long sidelong step into a thicket, hugging its shadow just as the horse broke clear of the trees. The rider lay flat to the mane, urging the animal into a reckless dash back along the creekbank, as Soderstrom had known he would. For the upstream country was boxed for several miles by ridges that made it impassable by horseback; a mounted man on the run would choose the open flats to the south.

When the horse was almost abreast of him, Soderstrom sprang from cover, sweeping back his clubbed rifle. Chad jerked upright in his saddle with a hoarse and startled cry. The sound snarled off in a breath-torn grunt as Soderstrom swung his rifle in a full-armed arc that just cleared the horse's head: the barrel caught Chad in a smashing blow at an angle across his belly and chest and shoulder. Soderstrom felt the solid ache of impact through his body, as the weapon was nearly ripped from his grasp. The horse thundered on past him.

Chad held his saddle, reeling, for perhaps six more yards, and then he toppled sidelong, the horse bolting on through the brush. Chad's body hit the bank and plunged down it into the shallow water. He was still conscious, making sobbing, half-retching noises. Soderstrom lowered his rifle, wearily supposing that he had crushed several of Chad's ribs. He slogged down the bank toward the downed man, guided by the roiling sparkle of water where he was thrashing feebly.

When a couple of the men had carried Chad back to the house, the sight of his son's condition had a considerable dampening effect on old Loftus' murderous fury. That, and Hannah's remonstrations: all other things aside, it remained that Chad had shot his brother in self-defense. Could Loftus shoot his son in cold blood—his one remaining son? Hannah, knowing her father, stressed this last part with some emphasis; nothing would finally gall a man like Loftus more than dying without a male heir. She was right. The thought put a sober punctuation to the old man's pawing and bellowing.

When Chad's four broken ribs had been securely taped, Loftus ordered his men to lay him in the wagonbed. Then, slowly and painfully, he heaved his massive frame up onto the seat.

Naomi sat beside him, her head down. She had, in a final burst of courage, declared her intention of leaving Wagontree and moving to town. Loftus was plainly not concerned one way or the other.

Sears' body had been tied across his horse, and the other men, already mounted, flanked the wagon, waiting to move out, but Loftus motioned them to get going. He had something to say, and he peered testily at Soderstrom who stood on the porch against the outflowing parlor light. He said, "You ain't won the pot yet, Swenska."

Soderstrom shook his head. "I won all I need, mister. It's you who wants to own the earth. No man can do that, Buckmaster. It will outlast even you. I think that's the big difference between us. I have felt for the earth as a man feels maybe for his woman, or for his kids. But you, to you it is like a big spread of food, and you have got to swallow it all."

"The hell with you," Loftus said, but a weary flatness had overtaken the granite rumble. "All right. I can't take on you and the government both. The U.S. marshal will be on my back for Crashaw's killing, I suppose, even if it was Sears done it. I never wanted that, but I've taken on the federal boys over land and water rights in my day, and I don't mind taking 'em on again." He tilted his head toward the back of the wagon. "And I got to get this thing I sired back on his feet and try to get him a short sentence. He ain't much, but he's all there is to carry on. I expect the devil will grant me the time I need to straighten some things out."

"I'd say you got enough trouble to keep you busy for all the time you got left," Soderstrom observed. "It is ended, then? The fight?"

"Our fight is." Loftus' iron-eyed glance shuttled to Hannah, who was leaning in the doorway, her arms folded. "I don't know about the one with her. I asked her to come see me now and then. What do you say, sister?"

"My opinion of you hasn't changed," Hannah said calmly.

"All right."

"I think you're a hard-hearted, bullying old tyrant, and I intend to continue saying so. But I'll visit you on one condition. Your door has to be open to Mr. Soderstrom, too, if you can resist making ultimatums—"

"The hell you say! Why should I let this goddamn squarehead set one foot across my line?"

"Because I'm going to marry him."

Soderstrom turned his head to look at her. His mustache stirred to his faint smile, and he glanced back at Buckmaster.

"Well," old Loftus said at last, dourly, "leastways you ain't spiting me this time. Are you?"

"Not a bit of it," Hannah said gravely. "This time I'm picking a rough, tough, honest-to-God shoot-out-their-liver-and-lights man like my daddy because I knew it would please you."

Loftus glared at her bitterly, and took up his reins. "Well," he said, "I don't like him, but finally I got a mote of hope for your good sense."

He shook the reins and clucked the team into motion, and

wheeled away into the shallow darkness. Soderstrom looked at Hannah again, and discovered that he could not say anything. There was a strange fullness in his throat. She said lightly, "Shall we go inside?"

They found McIver awake, weak and colorless. Thera had pulled a chair close to his bedside, and he was holding her hand.

"Only think of it," he was saying exultantly. "A few months ago, the wound alone would probably have killed me. Now, after being wounded, lying for hours in the rain, no dressing of any sort—why, I may be on my feet by tomorrow."

"Do not be foolish," Thera said contentedly. "Please stop talking now, David, and go to sleep."

Soderstrom stood in the doorway. He coughed abruptly, and they looked at him. McIver flushed, but did not let go of Thera's hand. "Perhaps you'd tell me something of what's happened, sir. I'm not clear on a good deal."

Soderstrom talked briefly for everyone's benefit, and his words left a sobering effect on them. The bodies of two men they all knew well lay out in the stable. "I'm sorry," McIver murmured, "for both of them. Waco was strange, and you couldn't really become close to him—but I liked Rafe."

"So did I," Soderstrom said brusquely. "But he had a mistake to pay for, and he paid."

"That was too big a price," McIver said shortly, and his hand tightened around Thera's. He met the older man's eyes defiantly. "I imagine you'll care no more for some of my judgments than I do for many of yours, sir. But you may have to get used to them, and I won't apologize for them."

"That's the least of our troubles, sonny," Soderstrom said with a grim satisfaction. "It ain't me you have to make the grade with. It happens my daughter likes caring for helpless things like you are now. But you wait, boy. You got farther to go yet than you know."

Hannah said good-naturedly, "Oh, come on, leave them alone, can't you?" She took his arm, and they went to the kitchen. "Sit down and watch, and i'll prove I can make a good cup of coffee."

"It better be good. A Swede can tell." He sat down, watching her movements as she laid a fire and set out the coffee-grinder. And he said quietly, "Why did you change your mind?"

Her busy hands paused, and she turned slowly from the stove. "I didn't, really. I knew what I wanted the first time you asked, just as I do now."

"You didn't see what you wanted before?"

"Oh, a lot of it. A woman wants marriage and a nice home and children and a husband who is clean and upright and a good provider. But first she wants a man, and she wants all of him. That's what you were withholding from me. That's why you couldn't speak of love. That's why I asked for gentleness. You've been living with too many ghosts, Krag, and they'd all but smothered the man I needed. With the gentleness, anything is possible—without it, nothing. The second time you asked, I still wasn't sure of it. But now . . ."

He got to his feet and came slowly to her, watching her face. "I am a rough man. Don't look for too much of it."

"I won't," Hannah smiled. "Just enough for a lifetime."

T. V. Olsen was born in Rhinelander, Wisconsin, where he lives to this day. "My childhood was unremarkable except for an inordinate preoccupation with Zane Grey and Edgar Rice Burroughs." He had originally planned to be a comic strip artist but the stories he came up with proved far more interesting to him, and compelling, than any desire to illustrate them. Having read such accomplished Western authors as Les Savage, Jr., Luke Short, and Elmore Leonard, he began writing his first Western novel while a junior in high school. He couldn't find a publisher for it until he rewrote it after graduating from college with a Bachelor's degree from the University of Wisconsin at Stevens Point in 1955 and sent it to an agent. It was accepted by Ace Books and was published in 1956 as *Haven of the Hunted*.

Olsen went on to become one of the most widely respected and widely read authors of Western fiction in the second half of the 20th Century. Even early works such as *High Lawless* and *Gunswift* are brilliantly plotted with involving characters and situations and a simple, powerfully evocative style. Olsen went on to write such important Western novels as *The Stalking Moon* and *Arrow in the Sun* which were made into classic Western films as well, the former starring Gregory Peck and the latter under the title *Soldier Blue* starring Candice Bergen. His novels have been translated into numerous European languages, including French, Spanish, Italian, Swedish, Serbo-Croatian, and Czech.

The second edition of *Twentieth Century Western Writers* concluded that "with the right press Olsen could command the position currently enjoyed by the late Louis L'Amour as America's most popular and foremost author of traditional Western novels." Any Olsen novel is guaranteed to combine drama and memorable characters with an authentic background of historical fact and an accurate portrayal of Western terrain.